About the Author

The process started with a Facebook short story sweepstakes, and through the process of completing the requirements for the sweepstakes, she fell in love with the story and continued to write. She has two young daughters and wants to inspire them to follow their dreams and believe they can accomplish anything they set their minds to. With that said, publishing has been her dream, and she is over the moon to see that dream actualized.

Deader's Day

Chasity Riddle

Deader's Day

Olympia Publishers
London

www.olympiapublishers.com
OLYMPIA PAPERBACK EDITION

A CIP catalogue record for this title is
available from the British Library.

ISBN: 978-1-80074-971-9

First Published in 2023

Olympia Publishers
Tallis House
2 Tallis Street
London
EC4Y 0AB

Printed in Great Britain

Dedication

I dedicate this book to my beautiful daughters, Jasalynn and Nichole. Always reach for the stars!

Acknowledgements

A special thanks to Richard, who has been such an amazing support, being my sounding board and best friend. Thank you for all the encouragement along the way.

Preface

For those of you who have been living in a hole and don't know what has been going on in the world over the last eight years, I'm here to open your eyes. My name is Anika Hart, and I started the revolution, with the help of a few friends. But before I get too far ahead of myself, let me back up and start from the beginning...

The year was 2056, the war had been over for a year, and the new world "Government" (who ironically call themselves "The Protectors") was in place, but in the rural outskirts of what used to be known as the United States, things were different. The states had been broken up into regions, and each had a sheriff who behaved more like a king. The sheriffs took direction only from The Protectors, and we, as civilians, reported to the sheriff. Moving regions was not allowed unless it had been ruled by The Protectors. If you put even a toe out of place, the death penalty was very much in force, and fear was our guiding star.

Water and food shortages had caused an even tighter ship. Ration supply had dropped and there were designated days for ration disbursements. Armed guards were there to ensure that no soul would take ration more than their allotted amount per family. The guards were put in place to show force and to aid in keeping the so-called "peace". The "state" issued blankets (gray woolen scratchy material that didn't help hold the warmth) and other supplies were only given out once a month, and those were sparse. The farms in each region were behind high guarded walls so no resources were stolen. You'd work for daily rations, but if you were late or didn't show up for work, ten out of the thirty days you were assigned, no matter the excuse, you would lose your monthly rations for a full thirty days (causing most to starve). If your attendance changed and you took on extra jobs, you could earn back your rations, but it was rough work. The sheriff could excuse your absence if you could get an audience with him and explain your case, but to my knowledge, this didn't happen often. We struggle with diseases of the blood, chronic pneumonia, infertility, and infection running rampant. You'd say, "Well we had all that post war, what's the difference?" and I'd say, "Not like this!" People all over the world over the age of forty are dying in a matter of hours after contracting the newest virus we call "Mid-Life". The term used for the victims of this disease are called "The Deaders" because there are no reported survivors. The Protectors created places for these victims in Auschwitz-esque holding centers to be "preventative" against the spread of Mid-Life. "Government" appointed people dressed from head to toe in hazmat gear would appear at your door on your fortieth birthday, also known as Deader's Day, and haul you away to one of these camps. It is not guaranteed that those individuals over forty would contract the disease, but they began rounding up everyone on their birthday to prevent others from contracting the disease. Most of the time The Deaders either leave their homes kicking and screaming in the arms of hazmat, or they leave in a black and red body bag and are placed into a matching Hazmat van. Deaders disposal sites have also been created, but most of the dead were cremated to prevent further spread of illness.

The original outbreak began in August 2048, the beginning of this war, when the original U.S. government regime was still active. A summit took place with a member from each of the world's governments, working together, they instituted a worldwide law that all citizens must wear gas masks, the first of many preventative movements implemented. The world governments issued these masks to children and adults alike. The CDC and healthcare workers didn't know anything about the virus in the beginning. With all the brightest minds working on finding a cure, everything was unknown, such as its origin and how it was spread. The only thing we knew was it became imperative we ensure the survival of the younger generations.

When the governments failed to provide a safe environment for citizens all over the world, the people went crazy, resulting in the rise of The Protectorate.

The new regime, The Protectors, stepped in, creating a new world order. The CDC, with the help of the Protectorate, put out a press release describing, in detail, and breaking down how diseases and viruses were spread (contact, droplet and airborne), then explained that Mid-Life didn't fit in any of these categories. Finally, they found more similarities amongst the victims, claiming that this disease only affected Deaders. The media went wild, broadcasting things like, "*People of the age of 40 and older are going to kill us all*" and "*The CDC found a link. What will the Protector's do now?*" This made it easier for the creation of the Deaders' camps and made it widely accepted by the masses– those under the age of 40.

After finding out Mid-Life was not airborne, the first thing the Protectorate did when they took power was removing the law that required gas masks to be worn; this calmed the nations, making them feel they were now in good hands.

Life was hard, and with our loved ones disappearing at an alarming rate, it was lonely, but this was before the revolution! My name is Anika Hart, and this is my story.

Chapter One

Anika

My life has changed so much. Like everyone else, I've lost loved ones and my sense of security. The world is no longer even recognizable to what it was eight years ago. The war started when I was sixteen years old. As a teen, I was a strong-willed, hardworking, and goal-oriented girl. School was difficult for me, though, and it didn't come easy; I had to work hard to achieve my 3.7 GPA. I also volunteered for my local senior center, babysat my neighbor's three-year-old daughter, Sophie, and spent the rest of my time with friends and family. I had a small, close knit group of friends, and I was really close to my parents. It is difficult to think about it now.

I used to go to the theater down the street from my school and watch all those post-apocalyptic movies. You know, the movies that have a worldwide E.M.P. knocking out all the power, or a deadly virus that wipes out half the world's population, or even movies about government takeovers and world war six. Back then, we looked at these movies as interesting to think about and all fun and games, but now, we look at them as educational training. Training for what the world has become.

Before Mid-Life, my dad, Adam, worked as a construction worker for a large company and my mom, Jeana, was a school teacher. Our favorite family vacation spot was the beach, going every summer. Having picnics and bonfires at night in the sand. We also would spend holidays with my grandparents on their property.

My dad was the first in my family to have his Deader's day, five and a half years ago on November 24th, 2050; it was so hard for my mom and me. My dad was our rock, our security and safe space. Shortly after Hazmat took my dad, the protectors relocated my mom and I to a new region, stationing us in a military-style barracks; it was stark and cold, nothing like home.

When my mother had her Deader's Day, she hid in our barracks basement for a week before Hazmat found her. The date was January 15th, 2052. My mom had no symptoms of the virus, but they took her anyway. As they ripped her out of my arms, she unclasped my great-grandmother's heart-shaped rose gold locket from around her neck (the one she had worn all my life) and handed it to me, just as they placed her in the back of a Hazmat van. I miss both of my parents so much.

I have kept the locket hidden deep under my military-style clothes to make sure not a soul can steal it from me. Personal items, other than region-issued, are prohibited. On nights that I am having a tough time without them, I pull out my locket and hold it in my hand, looking at my parents' faces and the "We are Mighty. We are Strong" engraving on the back. It comforts me, though, temporary as it may be.

The local area Sheriff, "Mr. Boss" as he is called, assigns residents in his area jobs, but they are limited. My job is to go through all the registered residents under Mr. Boss's rule and flag anyone coming of Deader's age. My only friend, John, is a twenty-eight-year-old Latin God; okay, not a god, but he sure is gorgeous. He is responsible for making sure that every resident is registered, so they can get food rations and other supplies. We work together hand-in-hand to make sure everyone is registered. In our area, we hold two of the most disliked jobs. Although, there are other employment options, such as sanitation; most people would consider it horribly disgusting—but in our community, they hate us more! They call us the "Snitch and the Tattle Tale".

With limited resources, employment is a luxury granting extra privileges, like extra rations and supplies; not everyone has an assigned job, but mostly everyone must pitch in to some degree. Not sure why I was given this responsibility when others would be better equipped. I hated my assignment so much. I had tried to give families a little extra time (the time I did not get with mine) by altering birth dates, but Mr. Boss caught some of the "errors". He did not seem to think I was quite smart enough to have made the errors, so he allowed me to continue my job after making a few changes to the process. Birth records are now kept with the files in the main office so no further "mistakes" can be made and double-checked by Cleo, an "elder" in our region who is thirty-five years old.

The town's population may be 11,928 today, but because of my job, there will be twenty-two less people with us tomorrow. If people don't start having babies, our population will soon dwindle down to nothing at this rate. We don't have much of a choice these days, though. The Protectors have now issued a new law called "The Pairing". The Protectorate has begun pairing the remaining population of earth from ages sixteen to thirty-two by region. Sixteen is too young in my opinion, but in our new world, they are adults. Pairing stations have been set up all over the world, a place that the paired couple can go to try to procreate. The pairing is supposed to guarantee that the population will increase quickly, or so we are told.

Speaking to John in our weekly meeting, he told me he was just paired with a little red-headed twenty-one-year-old named

Vicki, who bunks a few blocks away from me. John said their first "pairing" was extremely uncomfortable and felt unnatural, but because it is a law, they continued to do as they were instructed. He did say he liked Vicki and would like to spend more time with her. I have yet to be paired. I am so grateful for that fact; unfortunately, it's just a matter of time before I am.

My birthday is today. I am now 24. Instead of a party with cake and ice cream, friends, and family, instead of a celebration like it was when I was a child, it has become a countdown to Deader's day. To the end of the life I now have, to the camps, and ultimately to a brutal, gruesome death. We have not found a cure, or so The Protectors are saying. I, for one, think they don't want a cure because then they'd be out of power and control sooner than their own Deader's day and life could move forward without them.

I found a place up on the hill behind the recreation center that overlooks the town. I brought a bag with me that had a wool blanket to place on the ground and some rations to sustain me. Laying down on the blanket and looking to the bright shining stars, I begin eating my rations and hoping for a better tomorrow. As I sit here, I remember better times of my mom brushing my waist-length, curly brown hair, singing in my ear to the tune of our favorite Lauren Daigle song. My dad comes in the room and tells me, my eyes sparkle like the bluest ocean on earth and lifts me up, twirls me around; he was always the strongest man I knew… these are things they will never do again. I miss them so much!

Being submerged in my dream world, I got startled by a shadow in the distance coming towards me. It is past curfew. No resident is allowed to be out of the barracks between ten p.m. and six a.m., unless permission is given by the sheriff. I am bound to get in trouble. I tried to pick things up as fast as I could without being seen, but by then it was already too late; the shadowed person was upon me. As the light illuminated the shadowed figure, to my surprise, it was Matt, the mail carrier that goes from region to region and not a guard, to my relief.

Matt Harbrow is an average-looking thirty-two-year-old with no real characteristics that stand out. As the mail carrier, he is basically invisible and easily forgettable; no one really pays much attention to him or his whereabouts. I met Matt when my mother and I first were uprooted and planted here – wherever here is exactly is beyond me.

"Happy birthday, Anika." Matt said shyly. All I could do was bow my head and sulk. Matt handed me a letter. "It's from The Protectors," he said with a very doom and gloom sound to his voice.

As I assumed, it was my pairing letter. I fell to the ground and began to sob uncontrollably, wishing for a different time and place, where our lives were not dictated by a government overlord. As I lay there crying, Matt tried to console me by saying, "I have some good news, Anika. It's from one of the other regions. They may have found a possible cure!" Matt then handed me a spare piece of fabric to blow my nose with.

As I blew my nose and wiped my eyes, I asked, "Are you lying to me?" Looking at Matt with curiosity and frustration, then I said, "It is way too hard to believe that there is any possibility of there being a cure anytime in the near future!"

Still crying, he hugged me tightly and whispered in my ear, "I have also heard about something else, something that will truly change your life!" He hesitated for a moment, then said, "Your parents are both alive."

"WHAT?" I nearly screamed back at him.

Letting me go, standing and without another word, he literally ran in the opposite direction. I wanted to follow him, but he was well beyond the border before I got my senses back. Unsure if he was just trying to cheer me up or if he was telling me the truth, I was still elated at the possibilities. With my ugly, region-issued wool blanket, unopened pairing letter, and my rations in hand, I head back to my bunk. This was not how I wanted my birthday to go, but now I have hope.

Chapter Two

I woke with a start when the morning air horn blew, and my pairing letter was plastered to my face, and drool covered my pillow. I had to be at work in ten minutes, or I would lose my daily rations. Running my fingers quickly through my now shoulder-length hair, I patted my region issue clothes back down against my slim body, placing my pairing letter in my right front pocket. I ran out the door and literally right into Mr. Boss. He is about five inches taller than my 5' 7". He might be between two to three years older than I am, but no one really knows for sure. With dark brown abyss-like eyes that are now looking down at me and an amazing head of black hair that I struggled to resist running my fingers through it because it looked so silky. He had a body as hard as a brick (having literally just ran into him). I had bounced off him and landed in an undignified crumpled mess on the ground in front of Mr. Boss. Though he is attractive, I become crippled with fear and completely speechless. I have heard of people who have done less than this to our Sheriff who have ended up dead.

I repositioned myself to my knees and immediately began apologizing for my clumsiness. To my shock, he extended his hand to me. I reluctantly accepted. He had a strong, confident grip on my hand as he helped me stand with a curious look on his face; he was simply unreadable. I was still unsure if I was in trouble for my lack of physical awareness that I showed just moments ago or if he was going to let yet another thing slides for this "simple-minded" girl standing before him. His actions have become very unpredictable, and he doesn't allow much of a personality to shine through aside from the fearsome overlord of our town.

I was still standing in front of Mr. Boss, late for work and fearful for my life. Not a word yet spoken to me, and I'm beginning to become very self-conscious. Finally, he broke the silence and informed me, "Anika, I have been looking for you. You will accompany me on my walk." Abruptly he turned and started walking towards the governing compound. Completely confused, I followed behind him like a lost puppy unsure of itself and of its safety, tail firmly tucked between its legs. Turning his head towards me, he motioned for me to walk beside him; to my knowledge, this was taboo except for members of the government, which I am not, but not following orders could be my head. I reluctantly decided to walk a step behind him to follow protocol, but not so far behind him that he was offended either. Onlookers gave me very weird looks and the longer we walked, the more my head began to bow into further submission.

Mr. Boss escorted me to my office and left me at the door without another word. Fifteen minutes after he left, I received a note from one of the guards; it was for the rations board, excusing me for my absence and allowing me to obtain my daily rations. I was sitting at my desk with a large registration book propped open in front of me, I was unable to focus on my daily duties, reliving this morning events and trying hard to understand what had happened. The sunlight filtered in from the large picture window to my right. Subconsciously, I look around my stale office, hoping to find the answers I seek and the corner of my pairing letter caught my eye.

Removing the pairing letter from my front pocket, I sit and stare at it. I hate the idea of being paired with someone, much less someone I don't know, love, or even care about. This makes me think of the arranged marriages of old. I break down and grab a letter opener from my top left desk drawer. After unfolding the single gray sheet of recycled paper, I sit with my mouth gaping open; the words on the paper blur together. My ears begin to ring. I'm in shock, delirious; I must be losing my mind! This cannot be MY pairing partner!

Region 12 Area Sheriff, Mr. Boss

The next few days seem to run together. Work until the sounding air horn, then to my bunk. Sleep until I am abruptly woken by the air horn and repeat. Nothing of interest stands out. Daydreaming of the news Matt gave me with random flashes of the pairing letter. I'm consumed by confusion.

While at work, I found our town's population had dropped to 11,896, and that was with adding two new souls to the registration list. We are losing people at an alarming rate. Thirty people have been taken to the death camps in the last two and a half weeks, and only two souls added. At this rate, we will lose people faster than we gain them; there won't be anybody left before too long. It is mind-boggling.

Flipping through the registration roster, looking at the birth dates. 11,896 birthdates. It's a good day, though; I can take a deep breath and rest easy. I'm not sending Deaders to their death today! When I returned to my bunk, there was a note on my bed. The note was not signed, but it said some extremely mysterious words.

"He Picked You." was all that was written.

Living life in a constant state of confusion has become the norm. Could my parents truly be alive? Is it possible there is a cure for the Deaders disease? And that note, who picked me? Are they suggesting Mr. Boss picked me for pairing?

Chapter Three

Receiving another unexpected visit from Mr. Boss, he knocked ever so gently on my office door and stepped in. "Good afternoon, Anika. Due to my recent correspondence from the Protectorate, we have been instructed to appear at the pairing station on 15th street in twenty minutes."

"I will be ready in just a few moments. I have one more date to check before I can leave." I said to him, but in earnest, I didn't have another date to check; I was stalling. I was truly scared of the events that will occur at the pairing station. This is my first time….

Since I could stall no longer, I came around my desk and followed Mr. Boss out of my office door. Again, we travelled in uncomfortable silence, and I was yet again "asked" to walk beside him, to which I followed protocol and stayed behind him.

At the Pairing Station, it was not what I expected. I had envisioned a cold, dark and dreary, near-empty concrete building with bars on the walls, a grungy mattress on the floor and guards all around to ensure the law is being upheld, but instead, from the outside, it was kind of cozy and unintrusive to the eye. If you didn't know this was a Pairing Station, you would never have guessed.

Mr. Boss grabbed me by the hand and pulled me to the large, bright white door. He opened the door and we stepped into what looked more like a doctor's waiting room than the hostile imagery from my nightmares. We sat down and waited for our turn in silence.

After what felt like forever, the receptionist called our names, "Mr. Boss and Anika Hart?" She waited for us to approach the desk and then said, "You will be in room number six. Please follow me." After she ushered us back to room six and the door was opened to us, my jaw dropped even farther. It was a doctor's office! The reclinable exam chair in the center of the room, the wheelie chair for the doctor to sit, and the instruments cupboard were the only things in the room. Mr. Boss leaned against the outside wall facing the door after he motioned for me to sit at the exam chair. Only a few moments later, a grumpy-looking man in a white doctor's coat came into the room. He did not introduce himself but instead said, "Anika?" Once I nodded, the grumpy man grabbed my hand, harder than he should have and jabbed a needle into my arm, drawing blood.

"Hey, careful! That hurts!" I tried to jerk my arm back away from him, but he just grumbled inaudibly under his breath. He finished his job and then the unnamed man turned to Mr. Boss and repeated the process. "Mr. Boss?" I thought sarcastically to myself, "Like you don't recognize him!" As the doctor drew Mr. Boss's blood, he was much more gentle with him.

Once he had completed his job, he told us, "Leave."

Back in the waiting room, the receptionist motioned us to approach the desk, then informed us, "You will receive correspondence in a few days with the results." With that, we left.

John did say it was an "uncomfortable" situation and was unnatural. He never did go into any details; I guess I should have asked more questions. My assumptions ran wild, and I assumed a more perverted nature.

Mr. Boss silently walked me back to my office but this time he did not leave immediately. This time, he followed me into my office. I sat down at my desk, and he sat in the unstable chair in front of me. I kept imagining the chair collapsing under his weight. I had an extremely hard time not giggling at the thought. He then opened his mouth as if to say something but instead closed his mouth abruptly. Staring at one another in this very awkward situation without speaking was yet again making me extremely uncomfortable. Moments later, he once again opened his mouth to speak and said, "Until next time." Then got up, opened the door, and walked away, leaving me with my mouth wide, completely perplexed.

Instead of going directly to the barracks after work, I walked back to my favorite star-gazing spot only to run back into Matt. Matt looked around as if he was worried, fearful he would get caught talking to me. He repositioned his bag to his front and reached in to retrieve a small yellow envelope. He handed the envelope to me with a warning, "No one must see it, keep it hidden!" Only when I nodded in agreement did he release the envelope into my possession. In a moment of silence, I placed the envelope in my pocket.

I then turned to Matt and asked in my bravest voice, "What are the Pairing Stations really for?" Without a breath, I pioneered forward with all the questions that had been haunting me. "Why did they take our blood? I thought they were implemented to ensure more babies would be born…" Finally taking a small breath, and I ran my fingers through my hair absentmindedly. "I am really starting to question everything! And what you told me last time, please, tell me it wasn't a joke at my expense..." I said, cautiously watching Matt for any hint of the truth.

The only reply I received from Matt was, "In due time, you will understand it all!" pointing to the letter now stowed away in my pocket, then he said, "I must leave!" Off he ran. This letter must contain some seriously important information for him to be so abrupt and looking so paranoid.

I hid in the bathroom stall back at the barracks and pulled out the small yellow envelope. My name was inscribed on the outside, but something was off. The writing was extremely familiar and yet foreign.

I opened the envelope, enclosed was a two-page letter folded very tightly. I gently unfolded it to uncover my MOTHER'S handwriting. I slowly read the letter absorbing every single word, reading through watery eyes and being mindful that my tears didn't stain the pages. With this letter so much was made clear. Most of my questions had found their answers, but now there were so many others plaguing my mind.

I read the letter multiple times before finally folding it back up and returning it to my pocket. Stepping out of the bathroom and moving toward my bed, I turned and sat down, staring off in space, mentally working out the plan my mother had instructed me to follow. I looked at the clock; with only four hours before the airhorn will sound, I pivoted my body to lay down. Cradling my pillow in my arms, wishing I was hugging my mother in that moment, I whispered into the shadows, "Mom, I miss you so much!"

I was needing rest but all I could do was thinking about putting the plan into action quickly. Without much sleep the next day was going to be difficult.

Chapter Four

Mr. Boss came for me while I was at work. "Come with me," he said. Holding my office door open, waiting patiently, he shifted the weight of a dark brown satchel that he carried over his left shoulder.

"Where are we going?" As I asked him, I became irritated with myself for asking him anything as if I were entitled to the information. He just motioned for the door again. I then got up from my desk. All I could do was following in silence.

He had received the results from the Pairing Station but had not shared it with me. I would have assumed that I would have gotten my own letter with the results as well, but none came. He did not take me to the Pairing Station this time, though. As he walked, I just followed a step behind, as protocol dictated.

He led me past the ration's distribution hall, the recreation hall, and then down a small dirt walking path that had been concealed by tree branches, and finally, to an even smaller clearing. There wasn't anything around this empty patch of land, as far as I knew. Not a word had passed between us as I followed.

Once in the clearing, Mr. Boss knelt down on one knee and opened the satchel he brought to expose a blanket, a few rations and fresh fruit—the kind of fruit I hadn't laid eyes on in many years. I was trembling in my skin, a mixture of fear of being brought to such an isolated place with a man I didn't know, and a small amount of excitement that Mr. Boss wanted to spend time with me.

I knew I was getting ahead of myself with the feeling of elation over the simple idea of tasting a small amount of fresh fruit and thinking there was more to this "visit". I was, however, disappointed in myself because again I was only assuming that he brought the fruit to share with me.

After the blanket and the other items were placed on the ground in front of us, he motioned with his right hand for me to sit down. The awkward silence between us had caused the discomfort of the whole situation to settle into my bones.

Finally, he spoke with a calm voice that did ease my nerves just slightly. "The reason I brought you here is because it's private, without people to eaves drop." He took a deep breath and rubbed his five o'clock shadow with his left hand. I stood there wondering why it was he wanted to be alone with me. He then continued to speak with that calm voice. "I know what you did with the birth dates. I know you are not stupid, even in the slightest. You appear quiet to the general observer, but you are a witness to so many things. I fear you have already come into some truth, which may get you into trouble." Completely freaking out and expecting the axe to fall down on my neck, I began fidgeting and looking for the quickest escape root, when he swiftly spoke with his voice taking a more cautious tone. "I brought you here more to ask you for your help." Looking deep in my eyes, he said, "This must be kept quiet and between us for many lives are at risk! Will you help me? Will you help our cause?" His eyes began pleading for a reply, and he reached out and took both of my hands in his.

With my heart nearly in my throat and my breath excessively shallow, I was afraid I would pass out. The very idea that this was a trap had me on pins and needles. I kept my mouth shut, like it was being held in a vice grip. I simply nodded to appease him. He smiled at me with such accomplishment in his eyes that made me scared I had made a mistake.

He then handed me a small bunch of strawberries; to my surprise, tears began to fall down my cheeks as I put the fruit to my lips. I started remembering the warm summers, having picnics by the beach with my parents. Eating melons and strawberries, before my parents were taken from me, before the war and before The Protectorate came to power. An overwhelming feeling of sadness filled me, and I was unable to control my emotions. My silent sobs quickly erupted into the ugly crying that was accompanied with snot bubbles and horrible noisy gasps for air. Once in this state, the embarrassment hit and it became even worse, nearly hyperventilating.

Mr. Boss moved his body closer to mine and wrapped his arms around me to console me as I cried. He ripped his shirt and handed me the scrap of fabric to blow my nose. He seemed overly concerned and unsure how to act. Would he act as the Fearsome Overlord or would he be himself, the person he rarely showed to the outside world? "I am sorry for dragging you into this, but it is extremely important! I need your help." I could hear the honesty in his voice, and all I could do was nod into his chest.

Being wrapped in his arms, I couldn't help but notice he smelled of the wheat fields that used to grow by my childhood home. Earthy, familiar, and sweet. I began to sob even harder. He didn't understand why I was crying, and I didn't explain.

Tonight would not be a night for more words, no further conversation. Just the quiet noises of the bugs and night life. Once I had finally stopped crying and started random hiccups, we finished the rations.

As it was now well past curfew, Mr. Boss quietly repacked his bag and escorted me back to my barracks, again in silence, with me just a step behind.

Chapter Five

Diary Entry Anika's Mother, Jeana

January 26, 2056

My 40th birthday was supposed to be a milestone but when the virus was announced it became a day that I feared. 5 and a half years ago was the beginning of my family's fracture. The Hazmat team stormed our home and ripped my husband, Adam, out of the house and out of my arms. With a militarized government in place, they could dictate how we lived our lives and where we lived them. Uprooting my 18-year-old daughter, Anika and I from the only home we shared with Adam and placing us in an old military style barracks a hundred miles from what we knew in Seattle, Washington.

Shortly after the move, my birthday week was quickly approaching, so I found a way into the barracks basement cavity and hid. Anika would bring me rations to help sustain me, but it didn't take long for people to start questioning Anika as to my whereabouts. I showed no symptoms of the supposed disease. The symptoms were listed as: bleeding from the eye sockets, red blotchy skin, then developing large blisters all over the body, coughing uncontrollably until you start vomiting blood, all of this while having horrible diarrhea. Once you reached the vomiting stage, you would be just minutes from death. I had not seen a single person with any of these symptoms before or after the move to this retched city.

Before they took me away from my family, I was a second-grade schoolteacher. I looked out for everyone, and I would describe myself as very empathetic, but now the world has changed me and turned me callus and more jaded. I have been looking out for only myself for the last 4 years.

The extreme fear of the Deaders disease was gaining and resulting in the so called "Protectors" to take more liberties. Breaking families up, relocations, new militarized work camps, and then the implementation of the internment style camps for the Deaders.

The younger generation believed everything they were being told without question because the news and media had created such an extreme picture of what the world would look like if we did not remove the infected from the general population. The "Protectors" had been weaseling their way into the news and media long before the war truly began; it spread like wildfire in the other countries. When places like Europe, China and Africa were infiltrated, they moved to take over South America and the rest of the world, leaving the U.S. for last.

The Protectorate built camps quickly so as not to create suspicion amongst the general population. There are 3 main camps.

***The Internment Camps** - built to house the old and feeble Deaders. These people were given little food and were treated horribly. Eventually, they would die.*

***Labor Camps** - built to use the Deaders, the ones that were in good shape to work in the fields to supply the food rations. They also used them for other hard labor as they saw fit. They would treat them similarly to the Egyptian slaves.*

The Bio Camps - *these people were used as medical guinea pigs to test new biological warfare disbursement methods. These were pumped full of harmful drugs to watch and document the reactions to the various drugs and chemicals.*

I am unsure as to which camp they sent my husband to, but I just escaped from one of the Bio camps. I am looking for a safe place to hide, while I try to rescue my family from the grip of this horrible existence. With the medications still coursing through my veins, I struggle with constant pain and excruciating headaches.

Hiding in basements of old businesses, abandoned buildings and homes, even sewer drains if it kept me hidden from the guards and Hazmat teams.

Chapter Six

I was lying awake in my bunk, staring at the ceiling, unable to sleep as the dawn lightens the room, trying to process the information overload, I've received over the past few weeks. My mother's letter brought some clarity to many things with a whole barrage of new questions, and now that Mr. Boss has asked me to "help" him, I am even more confused than I was before.

Without even a wink of sleep, the air horn sounds, breaking me from my thoughts. I change my clothes quickly and walk to work. Rations day for me requires me to leave work at one p.m. and travel down to the distribution center.

Rations consist of powdered protein to be poured into water, energy bars that taste of cardboard, and, on occasion, they give a goop substance with the consistency of snot but tastes like cheese. The farms only give out fresh produce twice a month, and if you don't get to the distribution center early enough, they run out quickly. Most of the items are powdered or canned, requiring little to no preparation or cooking.

Living in smaller communities in close quarters, the chance of getting sick is much higher than a normal situation, so they also distribute vitamins and are strictly regimented, so the people don't fall ill. The paranoia that the Protectorate has created within our communities has instilled the severe need to stay healthy.

As I stand in line waiting for my box, I start to think about what food used to be like. Pizza, hamburgers, French fries, mashed potatoes with gravy, steak, fried chicken, and the list goes on, but for now, we deal with our rations and make no fuss.

Once I received my rations, I returned to work and place my box in the corner by the door. Moving around the corner of my desk, my eye catches a note from John asking me to meet him down by the water tower as soon as I was done at work. The next few hours drag by as I go through the registration book, one birth date at a time.

I stopped briefly by my bunk and dropped off my rations, and went to meet John. As I made my way to the water tower, I saw a group of three men huddled close together, whispering and every so often looking around with paranoia in their eyes. I kept my face forward; my steps quickened, and I acted as though I hadn't seen them at all but made a mental note of who these people were.

When I arrived at the water tower, I found John leaning against one of the stability poles looking at the sky. I made my presence known by clearing my throat so as to not startle him from his trance. His eyes fell from the sky to me as he straightened his posture.

John didn't waste any time in telling me why he asked for this meeting. "The test results came back for me and Vicki, and I'm really confused!" He then handed me the paper he had in his right hand. I accepted the gray recycled paper and began to read.

"*In the matter of John Freemont and Victoria Evercrest. This Pairing is now severed.*"

Nothing more was written on the paper, no other explanation. He turned his back to me and said, "I've gotten to know Vicki and really started to like her. I want to continue seeing her but now that the Pairing had been discontinued, does that mean it has become against the rules for us to see each other?"

Obviously distraught, I grabbed him and pulled him in for a hug and whispered in his ear, "We will figure this out! With this law being less than a year old, all the ins and outs have yet to become general knowledge to us all. I will do some digging and get back to you as soon as I have any news for you, okay?"

"Thank you, Anika! I didn't know where else to turn!" Hugging me quickly, he then walked me back to my barracks. Being that he was my best friend, I wanted to do whatever I could to help him out. There was only one place I knew I could turn to for this information.

When we got back to my bunk, we said our goodbyes and I walked inside. I immediately opened my WWII issue trunk and pulled out a piece of paper and a pencil. I quickly scribbled a note, asking what it meant for a paired couple to be severed and asked if the pair could remain pair, if there was any possibility. Then signed the note. Folding it in half and in half again, I wrote Mr. Boss's name on the outside and went to one of the guards that was stationed not far from my barracks and asked him to deliver it for me. The guard briskly walked in the direction of Mr. Boss's residence.

The next morning when I arrived at my office, Mr. Boss was already sitting in the unstable chair in front of my desk. I rounded the desk and sat down facing him. His eyes seemed much less scary today and seemed to have a sparkle of care escaping the dark lashes that framed his eyes.

"We need to talk but not here. Come on." He stood and motioned for me to follow him. I did as I was instructed and followed the same protocol and now habit of following a step behind. We ended our walk at the same place he had taken me for our picnic. Then and only then did he open his mouth. "What made you ask those questions?"

"I met with my friend, John, yesterday and he showed me a letter he got from the Protectorate that severed his pairing. He is really upset because he really likes the girl he was paired with." After explaining the events of yesterday evening to him, I pleaded for a sliver of information, "Mr. Boss, I would not be asking if it wasn't important to my friend. If you could tell me anything about this, I would be so grateful!"

He surprised me by being more forthcoming with information than I expected. Taking a deep breath before he said in such a matter-of-fact way, "The Pairing was not created to force partners to procreate but to test their blood for immunities against particular bio-chemical reactions." Without waiting for a reply, he kept going and said, "The Camps had not been built for what the Protectorate had said either. They have stolen people on a regular basis to use as lab rats and laborers for their own gain. The so-called "Deaders" were not all dead or dying from an unknown virus like they told us either." He then went on to explain the three camps that the Protectors had established. What he had told me was only confirmed by the letter my mom had sent me. The information he was giving just continued and left me feeling at a loss and extremely angry. With the information given to me by my mom and now Mr. Boss, this made me want to do something about it, anything at all.

Not wanting to appear vulnerable again in front of Mr. Boss, I let the tears prickle the back of my eyes but would not let them escape. I turned to him and asked him bluntly, "Why do you feel safe telling me any of this information?"

He replied with the most confusing answer yet. "You changed the birth dates!"

Mr. Boss

The day Jeana and Anika Hart walked into my region, I knew my life would change forever. Anika was truly the most intriguing girl/woman I had ever had the pleasure of meeting.

Putting beauty aside (which was hard to do at times), Anika was wise beyond her eighteen years. She approached every situation with true compassion; her intense loyalty to her family and even to those she had just met was mind-blowing. Though she put on an outward show of shyness around me, I knew with every fiber of my being that she was not shy at all or fearful of me as so many others were because of my position and reputation. She was respectful and demure. She had a strength to her that could command a thousand legions if only she opened her mouth. With just her presence alone, she made me weak at the knees.

I made excuses to see her in the early days of her arrival to Area 12. She rarely spoke or even looked me in the eyes, but I still visited. When I was told Jeana had not been seen in a week, I became worried for Anika and sent my most trusted guard to investigate. I was then informed by my Deader's Day reporter, George, that Jeana had passed her Deader's Day and had not been taken to the camps.

When Jeana had been located in her barracks basement, it was beyond my control at that point; the guards had removed her and three other people. I had found out too late that she had been found; the guards had already taken them to the Deader's Camps.

I kept my distance from Anika after this for fear of her hatred of me for sending her mother away. I made the choice to protect her the only way I could. When George was taken to the Camps, Anika became his replacement. Having a job would give her extra privileges and protections.

Growing up with a politician for a father, I knew nothing of true loyalty. My mother filled her days schmoozing with the women of high society, and her nights were spent bad mouthing those same women to my father at length.

My Father, Mario Emmanuel Woods the Second (grateful my parents didn't name me the third), was a very smooth talker, and because of this, he became the face and voice of the Protectorate in 2046. It was for this reason and this reason alone that I stand before you as the Region 12 Area Sheriff. My father's reputation within the Protectorate had made them "promote" me, not that I wanted the job, but to turn it down would have been an immediate death sentence. I knew too much! Now I need to help where I can to protect these people.

When I found out that Anika had changed the birth dates of some of the community to give them just a few more days with their families, I knew I could trust her!

Chapter Seven

Diary Entry Anika's Mother, Jeana

January 29th, 2056

The night that Hazmat took me from my daughter, I tried to fight to get back to my Anika. I gave one of the guards that held me captive a broken nose and what looked like a broken arm.

One of the people in charge took note of my strong will and instructed the guards to send me to be a guinea pig in the Bio Camp. The guard punched me in the stomach, tied my hands behind my back, blindfolded me, threw me in the back of another van and drove for what felt like an eternity.

Once we got to the desired destination, the guards dragged me from the van. With my face still covered with a blindfold, I could hear the sloshing of water on wet pavement and the clang of rusty doors as they opened and shut for us. The smell of mold, water, and the stink of bile engulfed my senses and made me begin to gag. The guards finally let me go but only long enough to tie me to a stretcher. I could hear them talking in muffled tones too quiet for me to make out what was being said just behind me. One of the guards laughed loudly, which echoed around the room. I heard footsteps heading back in my direction; only then did they remove my blindfold for me to take in my immediate surroundings.

The room I was in was more of a cell you would see in an old prison. There were bars on the high windows and a barred sliding door that closed off any escape from this foul-smelling hell.

I lost track of how long I had been there when, finally, someone in a black and red cloak came to my door and slid it open. Still strapped to the stretcher, my body ached, but even still, I tried to squirm and fight the cloaked figure as he stuck a needle in my arm. When he had removed the needle, the world began to spin, and I could not keep my eyes open. After I awoke, I had been removed from the stretcher and left on the cold, damp ground with a plate of slop placed just under my nose.

The next "visitor" I received stood at the closed metal door and shot me with a tranquilizer gun. Again, I crumbled to the floor unconscious, only to awaken with new bruises on my body, a plate full of the horrible slop under my nose and no recollection of time.

I kept screaming until my throat was sore and voice was hoarse, pleading for someone, anyone to let me out with no response. I was unsure of what they had been doing to me once they had knocked me out, but I was pretty sure it wasn't good.

Chapter Eight

With all the new information and the building trust being formed between Mr. Boss and I, things were becoming just a little brighter in my bleak existence. We began meeting a few nights a week. Once I got off work, we would meet in what we now call "our spot".

I have become, for lack of better terms, a spy amongst the people, rounding up all those who would support a revolt against the Government. I kept the names of these individuals to myself; trust still had to be earned, not freely given. I was not about to put targets on these peoples' backs, not after they put their faith in me. Still unsure of Mr. Boss and his intentions, I wanted to protect these people the only way I could, that is, until I felt truly safe to give him any real information.

Matt also would come bringing me more news of the other regions and the revolution being formed out beyond our "walls".

When I was still in school, I saw a painting of the Statue of Liberty bent over with her head on her knee, crying. I can only imagine if she were alive today, she would be doing just that. Crying for all the lost souls and crying for the condition of not only the United States but also for the world. I began sketching this iconic imagery as the symbol of our revolution. The symbol was to be secretly dispersed through the town's people and the neighboring regions, and hopefully becoming an image to unite us all once again.

I had one of the artists I knew, who started midnight tagging of buildings with our new mascot. Pamphlets were also created to hand to people and to send with Matt. Mr. Boss put on quite a show of surprise for the public and guards so, as not to arise suspicion. He was having staff to paint over the offending image, for it to be redrawn somewhere else, the next day. If the Protectorate ever found out that Mr. Boss was working on the side of the revolution, his head would end up on the nearest pike; they would make an example of him.

Every few weeks, members from other regions, people of power, would come to our town and see the "outraged" Sheriff. The sympathetic companions of these powerful people would take the image home to their territory and spread the word. Soon, Matt brought news that eight regions out of sixteen had the mascot popping up all over the area.

Returning to our place, Mr. Boss and I sat under the stars, talking about the accomplishments we have achieved over the last few months. "Mr. Boss, the plan is coming together nicely, but I think we need to take the next step."

Randomly he turned to me and said, "My name is actually Steven Woods. I'd like it better if you called me by my name. That is, while away from prying eyes and eager ears."

"Steven? Really, Steven?" I began taunting and teasing him, poking him in the shoulder and then in the side when he jumped up to chase me around the little clearing with us laughing uncontrollably. We ran around for a bit before he caught me and tackled me to the ground, ending with him straddling my mid-section and holding my arms above my head.

"My name is not that funny!" he said breathlessly.

When we realized the compromising position we were in, things became profoundly serious very quickly. Staring into my eyes, silently exploring the deep recesses of my soul, I became very aware of the feel of his body on mine and began squirming under his weight. As if he snapped out of a trance, he released me and moved to the other side of the blanket. Even though it was a cool summer evening, my body was now on fire!

"So, uh, it's starting to get late. We should head back." Steven said and abruptly started to pack things up.

When I made it back to my bunk that evening, I had visions of what life would have been like if Steven and I had met before the war. Envisioning introducing him to my parents, dating, and possibly even getting married and having children of our own. Dreaming of a happier time, but for now, I must focus on the task at hand. Now that the word was out, we had to put the next stage of our plan into action, but how?

Steven met me at my office the next morning, bringing with him the results of the tests from the Pairing Station and a new correspondence letter that he received earlier in the day. It instructed us to begin a regimented visit schedule to the Pairing Stations to commence IMMEDIATELY.

I asked quietly, "Do you know more about what the Pairing Station's grand plan really is, other than what you have already told me?" All he did was shake his head.

"They have left me in the dark as much as the rest of you on this matter." You could easily hear the frustration in his voice.

"With the knowledge about the Pairing Stations that you already have, why would they even ask you to participate in the process?" I asked but didn't honestly expect an answer.

"Unfortunately, I really don't know. I am just as confused as you are." He sounded almost defeated.

At this point, I asked about my friend. "What would happen

to John and Vicki if they continued to see each other, now that the Pairing Stations and Protectorate had severed their bond?"

Again, Steven was unable to answer the question. "I had assumed that they would have already been paired with someone new."

"I hadn't heard anything about a new pairing?" I just shook my head in disappointment.

We didn't continue the conversation but began our walk back to the Pairing Station as instructed, and, just like the first time we went, blood was drawn, and we were told to leave.

The receptionist gave us a brown paper bag, each with "new vitamins" in the bag on our way out. She then instructed, "You must begin taking these vitamins instead of the ones given to you at the ration's depot." She then called the names of another paired couple and walked away.

When we left the building, Steven whispered to me, "Stop taking all the vitamins," putting mini air quotes around the word vitamins. "God only knows what they really are. For all we know, they are trying to poison us." I just nodded.

We continued to go to our scheduled appointments so that we didn't draw any suspicion, all while trying to find a way to overthrow this Government.

Chapter Nine

With all the visits to and from Steven, I had not gotten a chance to visit John and see how he was doing in almost a month. I decided to take a few moments before I went down to the rations supply depot and find out how he was holding up.

John was sitting at his corner booth, seemingly staring off into space, waiting for people to come register when I arrived. He looked terrible. He had dark circles under his eyes and appeared to look as though he had not slept in ages. Instead of trying to break his concentration and announce myself, I went around the side of the booth and wrapped my arms around him in a gigantic hug. He jumped a little but soon realized it was me and embraced me in return. His eyes got red and slightly weepy as we pulled apart. I asked him, "What is going on, John? The last time we got the chance to talk, I told you the information I had gotten about the pairings. Is there something new that has happened?"

He turned his eyes towards mine but seemed to be looking through me rather than at me. With a single gesture, he pointed to a letter on the booth with his name on it. "Read," was all he could muster.

"John Freemont, you have been selected to be re-paired. Your new Pairing Partner is Gabriella Fredrickson. Report to your nearest Pairing Station for more details."

"When did you get this?" I asked.

"Two days ago. I can't make myself go! I miss Vicki!" he said with a crack in his voice. "I tried to go see Vicki about a week ago but when the guard saw me close to her barracks, he informed me since the pairing had been severed, I wasn't even allowed to be her friend. I am out of my mind, Anika. What do I do?"

I then told him to meet me at my star gazing spot at nine p.m., so as not be out past curfew. I would tell him the plan and hope that he would join us!

After talking to John, I went to meet with Vicki. Since we had never been paired, the guards did not have a problem with me going to visit. I told her I needed her to meet me at my star gazing spot, and I also instructed her to be there at nine p.m. Maybe this would allow me to tell them both at the same time and give them a moment to spend together. Fingers crossed that we do not get caught by the guards, since I decided that I was not going to involve Steven in this just yet.

At eight-thirty p.m.; I gathered up a few rations and a blanket in my bag, then headed out. I followed the shadows. Once, I could have sworn a guard saw me, but he went the other direction; I needed to pay better attention so I didn't get us all caught. Finally, after weaving my way up the small hill, I arrived and set up the blanket with the rations. I sat staring at the sky as I am waiting for the others to show up.

Vicki was first to arrive, and shortly after John appeared in the clearing. When their eyes met, they ran for one another and embraced. After professing how much they cared about one another several times over, I was finally able to sit the two of them down and discuss the real reason why I had asked them both there. The Plan.

We sat there and talked for the better part of two hours. We were able to get most of the plan worked out without too many flaws, but there were still a few other key people that needed to get in place before we could truly move forward.

Now that it was well past curfew, we had to sneak back to our respective barracks without getting caught. We said we would meet again in three days' time so that I could get a few things lined up.

During the next few days, John and Vicki would sneak up to the star gazing spot to be together. Even though they knew if they were found out that something terrible would happen, they continued. Their story made me think of the Romeo and Juliet story I read when I was in High School. Sneaking out to spend time with each other even though it was forbidden but loving each other no matter.

On the third day, I went to the lookout to wait for John and Vicki. John showed up, but Vicki did not. We waited for over four hours for her but still she did not show up. I left that night with a promise made to John that I would go to Vicki's the next morning.

At Vicki's barracks, I pulled the door open to begin investigating why she didn't attend our meeting, but found her bunk was completely cleared out. Not a sign that she even existed was left. I immediately went to John and told him what I found. The blood in Johns' face flooded out and down to his toes. John said gruffly, "We have to find her!" After I agreed to do whatever was humanly possible, he began pacing back and forth to the point I thought he might put a hole in the floor, imagining the worst-case scenario, and then paced some more.

I wrote a note to Steven that I needed to see him A.S.A.P., but before I could send it out, he was at my office door. He already knew of Vicki's disappearance. He was able to do some digging before he came to find me.

"Anika, please sit down so I can explain everything I was able to find out." He waited for me to have a seat then continued. "Vicki has been imprisoned by the Protectorate from what I was able to dig up. Due to the testing from the Pairing Station, they found that she is a carrier of a rare antigen that can break down most of the chemical warfare they have been working with." Taking a deep breath, he then said, "Which means, she could undo everything they are working towards. Still not quite sure what their end game really is yet, but we will find out." He finished reporting his findings and began to stare out my window with a very serious look on his face, then said, "If she truly could be the cure to whatever they are planning, then finding, saving, and protecting her needs to be our highest priority!"

Agreeing with him completely but honestly unsure where to begin, I start rambling every question that came to mind all at once. "Do you know where she is being held? If you do, how hard is it going to be to get her out of there? Do you think they will hurt her? Or worse, kill her?"

"I really don't know. I have not got a clue where they are keeping her. I already went to our regions' prison cells to see if she might be held there but no sign of her. The only real thought that I have is that they took her to Headquarters." He just kept shaking his head as he spoke, discouraged and disappointed in himself for not having more answers. "With Vicki having this rare antigen and being taken away quickly, we can assume we don't have the same antigen, but they are still interested in continuing their experiments on our blood." Running his fingers through his hair, he then said, “In so many ways, I hope they don’t find what they are looking for.” He turned his head towards me and the look on his face said it all. He had not even thought about that part of things.

He looked a bit white as I asked him, “What are they really doing?”

“We could speculate all day long but until we get to Headquarters, we aren’t going to know anything for sure!” With that we ended our evening in quiet contemplation.

The only other question I could even think of was where is Headquarters?

Chapter Ten

Putting the Plan to Action

Matt had become my "inside man", keeping me apprised of all the news he heard while in the other regions, and became my relay to the other growing factions of our revolution.

When I first lost my mother, Matt used to bring me things from my old house to cheer me up; of course, it has all been taken as contraband, but it was the thought that warms the heart.

I told him of Vicki and asked him to keep his ears open to her whereabouts whenever possible. I then asked the only question that had been rolling around in my head for the past few days. "I need to know where this Headquarters is located? How far are we from it?" If we had any chance of getting Vicki out and getting to the bottom of the plot of things, we needed as many facts as we could get.

Matt took out a small piece of paper and wrote a crude map of the area with the best way to get to Headquarters and handed it to me. "Headquarters is about seventy-five miles from here and it is impossible to get into without proper clearance. But I will do some digging to see how you can get in..." He trailed off in thought. Without a vehicle to make this journey, we would have to walk, and with the weather and terrain, Matt said it would take roughly six days to get there by foot and more than that to get back since the weather is about to turn.

After I stuffed the piece of paper in my pocket, I gave him a huge hug and thanked him for everything he was doing for us. As he walked away, he turned and said, "Anika, whatever you do, please be careful." I could see in his eyes that he was worried about me, but he knew once I got something in my head, there wasn't anything that would stop me. I'm stubborn like that.

A few days later, Matt came back and told me that Vicki had been relocated to one of the Bio Camps close to Headquarters to extract an antigen for study. He also gave me the guard's schedule of gates of days and times when the front gate at Headquarters will be mostly unarmed. This time when he left, all he could say was, "Once you are in, you are on your own. I don't have any one on the inside to help you!"

Steven and I had been getting pretty close over the past few months. With the weather turning colder in the late summer months, we had to look elsewhere to meet rather than our star gazing spot or the clearing, which was now getting the cold wind gusts from the west. We relocated to an abandoned barn on the outskirts of the region but not too far for the guards to take interest.

The barn was a tall two-story building with a loft and room enough for twelve horse stalls. The remanence of some tack was still on the walls in the tack room and shadows of old photographs stained the walls. The red paint on the exterior of the barn has faded with age and from the sun, pealing from half the boards, leaving a grayish, sun-bleached color underneath. There were still some hay bales strewn all around the upper level and hay on the floor of the stalls. We managed to grab a few bales from the upper level and create a sitting area in one of the stalls to create a little bit more warmth on the cold nights.

Talking with Steven, my mind wandered and went on quite a tangent thinking about how, when the Protectorate came into power, all the livestock were seized, saying maybe the livestock had been infecting our people. I soon came to the realization that they took the livestock to make it easier to control the food supply and to reinforce their "we have your best interests in mind" movement. Once they were gone, gas became a rare commodity. With most of the farmers' equipment no longer able to run, they had no choice but to leave, abandoning their farms and relocating to wherever the Protectorate told them to go, or the farmers would starve.

The smell of the sweet, warm, earthy hay brings me back to reality and back to Steven, who seems to have been talking the entire time I was daydreaming. I am completely at a loss as to what he is saying at this point and feeling embarrassed that I must ask him to repeat himself.

"Steven, please forgive me, my mind seemed to have wandered off and I honestly didn't catch anything you were just saying. I am so sorry; can you please repeat yourself? I am back, I promise!" I begged him, feeling sheepish.

"Sure, what was the last thing you do remember me saying?" He looked a bit annoyed, but his voice didn't hint at it even a little bit.

"Well, I think you were talking about my mom's letter." I looked at him hopefully. "And how she told me to go to Headquarters to steal some paperwork for proof, but you said it was too risky. How far past that had you gotten?" Still embarrassed, my posture was almost cowering in on itself, eagerly awaiting his reply.

Looking a bit shocked, he said, "Actually, you didn't miss much." With this being said, my posture grew a little straighter and less embarrassed. "I just said with Vicki being taken and for the reasons she was taken, I was going to agree with your mother, but I wouldn't be able to go with you. I have to stay here to save face; I'm still this area's Sheriff and need to appear to the Protectorate that I'm doing the job, you know?" Grabbing me by my wrists so I pay close attention to what he is about to say, he blurts out, "I want nothing more than to go with you, to protect you, to help you, and to find out what else their hiding, but I can't!" He then slides his hands down my wrists to hold my hands. He has become much more affectionate as the months have gone by. I'm not sure if I am imagining things, wishing for more or what.

With our hands still intertwined and fire growing in my stomach, I say, "I understand. Matt gave me a crude map of how to get from here to there. In Mom's letter, it had the blueprints of inside Headquarters, so, the plan is pretty sound. It is now just a matter of getting there that is the problem. With winter quickly approaching, this is going to get difficult if we don't put this plan into action soon. John volunteered to go with me, so I won't be alone. I have protection. I will be okay!" She was trying to remind him of the severity of the weather and ease his mind in the same token, but I'm not sure if I did either.

Chapter Eleven

John and I had started a workout regimen about a month ago so we could make the journey without too much of a struggle. To increase endurance and strength, we started running from my barracks to the star gazing spot and back. At first, the guards freaked out, thinking we were trying to run away, but as soon as they realized we were just going back and forth, they calmed a bit. After a few weeks of this, they didn't pay us any mind. At night, we would pack away what we could and what we felt would help us along the way. Rations were enough to last for the estimated twelve-day trek with a few days extra, fire starters, water purifier, warm clothes, and a few other things. Looking back at this, we should have packed more and thought more about the impending weather, but I guess that is the old saying hindsight is twenty-twenty.

During our time together, John would tell me a bit about his life before the war. His school-teacher mother and his alcoholic father. How much easier his life had been when he would just follow instructions, didn't talk back, or stray from the 'Plan'. He had few friends as it was easier and less embarrassing than having to explain his home life to others. With his mother at school with him making sure he didn't say anything about what was happening behind closed doors, friends were just a luxury he couldn't afford to have. So when the war hit and he no longer had his parents over his shoulder, he followed the same path of least resistance, which landed him the job of Global/Region

Registration Recorder, or GRR for short, since it is quite the mouthful. He said, "When the war started, I had just turned twenty, and I had been making a name for myself as a loyal lacky. The Protectorate saw my 'potential' and that is how I got the job." He no longer wanted to be that person, the person that follows everything they are told without question; he wanted to finally step out of the shadows and do what was right. Accompanying me in this "quest" was his way of doing just that, and to find and protect Vicki the way he couldn't do for his mother and to help ensure my safety in the process.

On one of the warmer nights, we decided to go to the star gazing spot to just relax and recoup from all the stress. John lay there quiet for quite a while before he finally spoke.

"I grew up in a small rural town in the middle of Oregon. My father had made sure I was in boy scouts, taken fishing, hunting, foraging, camping, and was involved in any kind of wilderness survival training that he could get me into. My mother, being a teacher, was very soft spoken and demure in nature. She had been more or less beaten into submission by my father, so she went along with whatever my father said.

On one of my father's bad nights, he had already put away a twelve-pack of beer and was working on a pint of whiskey, and he decided he needed to teach me to be a man. A man that was strong, capable, and ready for anything. He loaded the pick-up with a tent, firearms, and a boatload of alcohol. Then he took me out into the middle of nowhere in Mt. Hood National Park (still drunk, mind you), swerving from white line to white line until we got to 'the spot' where there was nothing and no one for miles, then set up camp. Once we got a fire started, he was high on his soapbox, preaching to me about what it meant to him to be a 'real man'. It was always hard to follow his rants when he got that drunk, between the slurred words and asking for more to drink. That night, he hit me across the face because he didn't believe me that he was out of alcohol. Once he investigated for himself, he finally made his way to the tent and passed out, leaving me to have some peace and to commune with nature without his ranting voice in my ear. On that night, like so many other nights, I sat there with a gun in my lap staring into the firelight, feeling the sting on the side of my face, thinking of ways to end him, to make my mother and I's life so much better, but I never followed through.

When he awoke the next morning, he had a raging hangover and little to no patience level, all while being pissed he was out of booze. After he loaded up the tent, he grabbed a gun and told me to grab mine and follow him. As we walked, he pointed out several different kinds of mushrooms that were edible, such as the Shantelle and Morel mushrooms, and some different berries that you could eat, like the salmon berries and huckleberries. We walked for about twenty minutes when my father abruptly stopped in his tracks and told me to wait there, that he had forgotten something in his truck. Doing as I was told, I stood there watching, waiting, and listening, only to hear my father's truck start up and drive away. I was left with relatively nothing but the clothes on my back, a bottle of water, a pocketknife in my front pocket, a few bullets in my jacket pocket, and my .22 rifle in hand. Standing there in true shock that he had just left me.

It took me three days to make my way to town. I had foraged in the forest along the way so as not to starve and made primitive shelters at night. When I walked into the Sheriff's office and told them what had happened, Child Protective Services got involved since I was only twelve at the time. Apparently, my parents didn't even put out a missing child report, and my father didn't even come looking for me. He went on a three-day fishing trip off the Columbia River, and my mother assumed I had been with him. CPS put me in care in the next town over from mine, but I was soon home because they couldn't 'find any evidence of neglect'. CPS knew there was, but because they could not find hard evidence other than my word, they had to close the case.

Life got even harder after that. Since my father couldn't get rid of me by leaving me for dead in the middle of nowhere Oregon, he began beating my mother and I more frequently. He changed his tactic in saying, 'if you don't do this, I will kill your mother.'

School became the same for me, do as your told or I will… so, I became an extreme follower, never a leader. A yes sir or yes ma'am guy. Never sticking up for myself or sticking my neck out for anyone else for fear of the beatings and what he would do to my mother.

My father's drunken antics eventually got him killed when I was seventeen. He wouldn't leave well enough alone when he was drunk, picked a fight with a local guy at the bar and got pummeled to death in the back-alley parking lot – six guys helped. It was a relief for my mother and me. We were free. I was finally able to escape from that life, but by then, I was willing to do anything to find approval from others.

After I moved out of the house, my mother had no one but me, and, with years and years of abuse, the depression, fear and regret had taken its toll on her. She refused to eat and drink. She started hallucinating that my father was around every corner. I came to visit her and found her crying in the fetal position and unable to speak. I called 911. Once at the hospital, they admitted her into a long-term psychiatric facility. That was the last time I saw her. I attempted to visit several times, but she refused to see me.

I was then contacted by my mother's brother, James, who wanted to help me. Now that my mother was in a facility and my father was dead, the city was saying if I am unable to pay the mortgage on the house, I would lose it. James offered me a job as an accountant at a big-time firm so that I could pay the bills. Even though I hated my job, I was really good at it. I moved up the corporate ladder pretty quickly and met with a few of the big wigs of the Protectorate soon after I turned twenty. And well, you know the rest."

We sat there quietly for a long while; I had no idea what to say to him. He had been through so much in his relatively short life. I felt for him but was still speechless. Now that I know more about him, it explains so much. Why he fell so hard for Vicki and so fast, why he is so gung-ho about going after her and protecting me, and why he was so intent on proving himself. He is so much stronger than he will ever know. I am grateful to have him with me on this new journey.

Chapter Twelve

Diary Entry Anika's Mother, Jeana

February 2nd, 2056

I'm becoming more and more sick as the days go by. My body is showing signs of what they did to me in the Bio Camp. I ache all over, extreme fatigue from lack of nourishment, and rations seem nonexistent. I've been able to find some food in the abandoned houses, but most of it is well past spoiled.

I found some clean clothes in one of the places I hid for a night and was able to wash up, which did lift my spirits some. Although, when I got out to change and looked down at my body, I saw the weight loss and the green illuminated veins starting on my chest and migrating out towards my stomach. Whatever they injected me with at the Bio camp is starting to progressively get worse. I have to speed up my search for my family before I can no longer move.

Today, I finally caught a break. I ran into Matt, a familiar face from a lifetime ago. He was someone I met many years ago when the Protectorate relocated my Anika and me. He became my very good friend. Being a mail carrier allowed him to cross region lines, so I gave him a letter for my daughter and pleaded with him to bring it to her for me. I explained everything I knew in that letter, all the truths that were going on out in the world.

Dear Beloved Daughter,

I am still alive and looking for your father.

When they took me, I was taken to a camp called the Bio Camp. They test different biochemical drugs on everyone; the weak don't last even a day there, but I was able to make it a year until I escaped.

The place I was able to discern where they took your father was a Labor camp just north of Headquarters. They put the people that appeared to be weak and feeble into The Internment camps to die from malnutrition and starvation, people with a strong back and endurance into Labor camps, and those of us who have a strong will that wouldn't work in a Labor camp into the Bio camps.

You, my love, have a part to play. I hate to ask this of you, my dearest daughter, but we have no other options here. You need to go to Headquarters and steal all proof of what they are doing. Distribute it to all the regions and try to recruit as many people as possible to help you along the way. The people need to know what the Protectorate is really doing. They are a small entity that appears much larger than they really are. You can do this.

Attached is a blueprint of the Headquarters and where to find what you need. I have been able to find quite a bit of information on my own, but I was only able to get a small fraction of what we need to stop them. Get the word out to the world!

I love you with everything I have! Always remember that! I am with you always!

Yours always,

Mom

Chapter Thirteen

Steven made it known to, well, everyone, that he was having John and I worked on a special project, and we would not be seen at our post or at the Pairing Stations for two or three weeks. This potentially enabled us to go to Headquarters and return without any one questioning our disappearance. He stated that this project that John and I were on was of utmost importance to the protectorate, and as soon as it is completed, we will return to our scheduled appointments as usual. Most of this was not a lie, so it was believable when he said it. Even though Steven told this to the guards, we still didn't want to get caught by them leaving the region lines.

Saying goodbye to Steven was difficult and made awkward by his constant touch, making me feel warm in my stomach, and his reassuring words that everything will work out.

"Instead of saying 'goodbye,' let's just say see you soon! You will find everything we need to take them down. I have faith in you! Make sure you stay together. Keep each other safe!" He nearly crushed my ribs when he squeezed me around the waist.

John and I grabbed our supplies and left under cover of darkness. We walked quickly past the region line just shy of two of the guards spotting us, making my heart fall so fast I thought I would throw up. The first day was spent mostly by looking over our shoulders. Once we made it into the trees, we were able to finally take a small breath.

The weather took a turn for the worse with a torrential downpour on the second day. With our bodies soaked to the bone, and our temperatures declining quickly, we needed to find or make a shelter and get a fire going as soon as we could. We Found a downed tree with the root system that created a cave-like area. We used it for shelter and huddled up close to the fire to bring our body heat back up. Once we get to more populated areas or closer to region lines, we won't be able to use a fire, so it was a small luxury we relished this night. We ate a small amount and rested for another long day ahead of us.

The next two days, we didn't run into too much trouble. Most of our days were spent walking in secluded forests. We were able to find shelter with ease, but we had a canyon in front of us and a river to cross with a guard shack on either side to tackle. We set up camp for the night and tried to make a plan of attack. We had no weapons to take on the guards, and, even if we did, they could radio ahead to other guards for reinforcements. Being stealthy was our only option.

"This plan is making me feel like a never-ending game of Sudoku and none of the numbers are lining up right!" I exclaimed in total exasperation. "How are we supposed to get through this with little to no supplies left? I am seriously second guessing my skills. What have I contributed up to this point? I have to get this information from Headquarters, not for me, but for the world!"

"I think you are putting too much on your shoulders, Anika! You have done well so far, and we will get to Headquarters!" John rubbed my right arm in a show of support and comfort, but it did little to help my nerves.

I say in a choked voice, "I'm really worried that we took this on too quickly, that we didn't think of what we would really need out here." The tears began to prick the backs of my eyes. "We are running out of supplies, and we don't have any weapons to protect ourselves with! It is only going to get worse when the weather gets colder, and we won't be able to forage." I begin to cry a little but mentally kicked myself for being weak at a time like this.

With the most comforting voice John could muster, he said, "We will just have to make sure when we do find food that we hoard what we can. We will make it! Though my father was a horrible person, he did give me a lot of skills. When we get closer to rivers, I can make a trap for fish and, in the prairie lands, I could make a makeshift bow and arrow to get smaller game. We will be okay!" Then he gave me a hug that enveloped all my fears and threw them to the wind.

It has gotten colder sooner than we had expected. and our supplies have dwindled so quickly than we could afford. John is scrambling to find us something to eat with little luck. With all of his survival training, I trust he will find something soon.

Sitting on a log, looking out towards the canyon, I tell John everything I observed while he was out looking for sustenance. "After watching the guards, they switch shifts mid-day and are a lot less attentive to their surroundings at shift change. We could make it past one guard shack and through the river without being noticed, but the second set of guards would have had time to get report and settle in. Crossing here does not seem to be our best option."

He looked at me with a lightbulb-over-his-head moment and said, "While I was upstream a bit scavenging for food, I found a downed tree that went over the river. We would be able to cross there and bypass the guards all together," he said with more confidence shining in his eyes. Luck may yet be on our side, but I will not count my blessings. We still have to make it to

Headquarters and back!

As we were walking toward the downed tree that John was telling me about, he stopped abruptly and let out a small gleeful noise. "Ha-ha, look Anika, I just found some miner's lettuce and over there, look, there are some dandelions," he said, pointing in another direction to our right. "I know this doesn't look like it, but it will be a really good salad mix! I'll get the miner's lettuce. You go over there and grab the leaves of the dandelions and some of the flower heads. I can make a plate from this bark!" He seemed so excited by this find. I did as I was told and brought him the ingredients that he asked for.

"This is really kind of bitter," as I ate what he put in front of me.

Agreeing with me, he tried to reassure me, "Yeah, I know, but it is really good for you!"

I ate another bite. "Thank you, John, for keeping your eyes open." Flashing him my best smile, I said, "I would be lost without you!" Though this salad fed us, it was not very filling, and we burned it off pretty quickly.

Chapter Fourteen

Once we got to the downed tree, I was really worried about walking over it. "Are you sure it's safe?" Apprehensive to make the first step, I said, "Do you think it will fall if we put weight on it?"

"I have already tested it to make sure we would be okay. The only thing is, if you feel like you are going to fall, sit on the log and scoot across. It is safer to do that than to fall in the water." Holding out his hand to help me onto the tree, I took it and pushed forward.

"Okay, here goes nothing!" Choosing to push my fears aside for another day, I took one step after another until I had finally made it over the river and back onto solid ground. I did a little happy dance, to which John started laughing at me.

"What is that?" he said through his laughter. It was the most beautiful sound I had heard in, well, forever!

"I made it! I was excited!" I started laughing with him, and he just laughed even harder. It felt so good to finally laugh. Even though this was a stressful time, this was desperately needed.

A few miles past the log bridge, I was yet again stopped abruptly by John and his foraging skills. He found something called bitterroot, and it was exactly what the name described, bitter. With little to no food rations left, I took what I was given.

"Why is it that everything that is good for you either tastes like nothing or it is excessively bitter?" I feel as though I have turned into a food snob and had begun whining whenever he was able to supply some kind of sustenance. I will have to work on sounding much more appreciative in the future.

He looked at me in complete contemplation. "You know, I really don't know the answer to that! Maybe I can look for something that tastes a bit better rather than all this bitter stuff, but for now, we have something that will keep us alive. Let's eat." John looked down at the bitterroot with just as much disgust after he took another bite and said, "No matter how gross it is, just remember it is good for you."

I nodded and continued to muscle through eating as we walked. The hill we had been walking for the last mile was finally starting to level out, but fear shot through my bones as soon as the clearing was in view.

We found what used to be a town. The place was falling into disrepair, the roads cracked with weeds growing out of them, the paint on the buildings faded with plants growing up the sides; it was so depressing.

"I think I have been here once with my mother, back from before. It all looks familiar and yet different." I looked around, eyes wide, mouth gaping. All John could do was nod.

It felt like we were exploring a foreign land on a planet way off in space rather than the world we now live in. Eight years without people has made this place feel like an empty shell from a time long lost.

I looked around this deserted town, completely taken everything in. A fluffy brown cat darted from behind a nearby building and startled me. It ran from one side of the street to the other and vanished from sight. I jumped back slightly when the cat jumped out, with John there to brace me. "Everything is okay, it was just a cat, Anika, just a cat." Comforting me seemed to be his second job. I appreciate him more and more every day that we are out here. I could not ask for a better friend if I ordered one in the mail.

Taking a deep breath, I wandered into what looked like it used to be a diner. "Come here, John, maybe they have non-perishables in the back that we can eat…" I trailed off after I opened the door. The tables had plates with what used to be food still on them, chairs turned over like they had left in a hurry, and the smell of mold overwhelmed my senses. "What happened here?" In complete awe of what my eyes were seeing. "Do you think The Protectors just scooped everyone up from where they were and made them leave? Because that is what this looks like to me!" I looked at him briefly and then back to the scene in front of me.

"Honestly, that is what it looks like." He started wandering through the tables and picked up a fallen chair that was in his way. He remained in the bent position looking at the floor before he called out, "Look over here, Anika," pointing to a small, slightly shiny thing amidst the dust and dirt on the floor. "It looks like a bracelet…" He picked it up and dusted it off the best he could to reveal an engraving, the same saying that is on my locket.

"I know that saying! Here let me show you." I reached under my shirt and pulled out the rose gold locket and showed him the inscription on the back. As I had said, they matched.

"Well, my dear, it looks like it is your lucky day. You now have a match to your locket." He had me extend my arm out and placed the fragile-looking metal on my wrist. Just looking at it made me smile.

I almost jumped into his arms, "Thank you, John!" Giving him a big hug. "You have no idea what this means to me!" Embarrassment flooded his cheeks, and he looked away.

As he pushed me off, he changed the subject quickly by saying, "All right, let's head into the back to see if there is food or not." He moved swiftly towards the kitchen area, not looked back at me.

In the kitchen area, there was a walk-in fridge and freezer to our left, and to our right was what used to be the produce bins, now covered in growing plants that did not resemble anything I had seen before. Nothing edible grew from them.

"I'm afraid to look in the fridge and freezers. Since there isn't any electricity here, I can only imagine the smell that would come out of there. I don't know about you, but I don't feel like puking today," John said as he avoided the area completely.

I looked at him with disgust. "I'm having a hard enough time keeping that bitterroot down as it is, let's not talk about puking, okay? I agree, though. Let's steer clear of that area and look for the dry good storage, that is, if there is any left." Looking around, I did see a few things that would come in handy on our trip, like a few metal plates and utensils, which I put in my pack, but I didn't see any food.

John started opening cupboard doors and investigated the contents before moving on to the next one. "Find anything?" he asked when he closed yet another cupboard door.

I had been in the hallway when I heard him ask. "I found it, I think..." I opened another door leading off the kitchen; sure enough, it had been where they had the dry storage, but it looked like it had been ransacked. John came running and seemed just as disappointed to see what was left of the contents. A few cans of green beans and a moldy gravy mix container was all that was on the shelves. The floor was littered with remnants of rice bags that had been torn into by what appeared to be rodents. Well, at least the cats have food.

John grabbed the green beans, and I went back into the kitchen to look for a can opener when we hear a noise coming from outside. “Stay down!” John whispered the demand, and he crept toward the front window to see what the commotion was. Just as we feared, the guards were doing a patrol of the area.

I whispered, “Go out the back!” pointing to the back door. Opening it as quietly as we could, we crept out, down the back path to a storm drain and stayed there until the guards passed. From now on, we would have to do a better job of keeping ourselves out of sight. I couldn’t imagine coming all this way only to get caught and sent to God knows where without completing our mission.

Chapter Fifteen

As we made our way out of town, John found some weird plant that was growing out of the crack in the pavement that he called knotweed. "The whole plant is edible, but the seeds, here," he said as he bent down to pull off some of the seeds to show me. "These are the better part of the plant." He grabbed several handfuls of the seeds as we walked and began eating them.

We walked back into a wooded area just outside of town, and John said, "I, myself, need to make a quick detour!" and ran for the bushes. It had only taken an hour or so before the seeds had affected him in such a horrific way. Not too much further down the path, all I heard was him say, "Oh God, not again!" He disappeared into the bushes faster than I could say diarrhea.

In small doses, the knotweed seeds are fine, but in John's case, he chose to eat far too many, and they gave him violent diarrhea, and he became severely dehydrated. Due to this, it slowed our pace quite a bit. We traveled in silence, and it was hours before we were finally able to get up to speed again.

John finally broke the quiet contemplation I was having and said, "I should have known better, I'm sorry for slowing us down." His words came out dry and hoarse.

"It's okay, John. How are you feeling now?" Turning to him, I asked with honest concern in my voice. "Here, have another drink of water. It should help." I pulled a water canister out of my pack and began handing it to John.

He held his arms around his waist and replied, "My stomach

is still doing cartwheels but other than that I think I will be okay." Taking the water from my hands and taking a long drink, he then said, "Thank you, Anika." His voice sounded much better. "That helped."

"Do we need to stop for the night?" I asked as I began looking around for a suitable place to bed down for the evening.

He shook his head and said, "No, I'm okay. Thank you for your concern, but I have already slowed us down too much already." The frustration on his face was almost palpable.

"I think maybe we should stick to the food we know a little better, so this doesn't happen again. Agreed?" I tried to be sympathetic, but being honest with myself, I was actually rather annoyed that we had been going so slow and made such little progress. The trip was only supposed to take twelve days both ways, but with all the complications, it is going to take far longer than that.

"Agreed," was all he said to me. John knew that if this would have happened when he was younger, he would have gotten the beating of his life from his father. Trying to shake it off and get his head back, he began to move faster to gain some ground before setting up camp. Still not feeling a hundred percent, he began an internal mantra of, "I can do this, I can do this," over and over until he was finally able to pick up speed.

We were trying to decide if we should get some sleep as the sun was coming up over the small ridge in front of us when we heard a noise.

"*Shh.*" John was now crouching down into a thicket when he pulled my arm down hard so I would join him.

"Ouch, what was that for?" I scowled at him as I was now sitting in wet soil.

"There is a large black bear right over there." He pointed just up the path from us. "We need to be quiet, so he doesn't hear us...*shh*!" While not looking at me, he put his pointer finger to his lips.

He was looking through the thicket in the dawn light, seeing the bear devouring a bush that had berries on it. John yet again whispered, "Those are salal berries. If the bear leaves us any, we really need to grab some. They are sweet and would be a nice change to the bitterroot!"

I just kept imagining the bear hearing us talk or catching our scent and devouring us as dessert. I chose to say nothing in reply so as not to let my insecurities and fears run rampant.

Once the bear left, John went to go get the remaining berries. I stood up from the thicket I was sitting in and started walking toward him. The ground gave way under my feet, and I went tumbling down a small hill into the middle of a stinging nettle patch.

My mother used to drink a tea with stinging nettle leaves in it, and I did find I liked it, but falling into the middle of them was not so much fun. I had to wade through the patch before I could start the upward climb back up to where I left John, but this hurt. I remember my mother telling me not to touch the sores with my bare hands because the oils on my hands would cause the sting to intensify, and she had been right. With every step, the leaves would brush my face, my hands, or poke through my shirt sleeves and make me wince.

Panicked, John cried down the hill, "Are you okay? Did you break anything?"

Anika said, "Just my pride. I landed softly in the middle of a stinging nettle patch." I was trying to make a joke at my own expense so as not to start cussing at myself for doing such a dumb thing. I yelled up the hill at John, "I had forgotten how much these boogers hurt!"

The climb back up the hill wasn't very easy either. The ground was still wet, and with every step, my foot would lose what little bit of ground I had gained. "Crap!" I groaned in frustration as I fell back to the ground and back to where I started. "There has got to be a better way!" I said to myself.

"Are you all right, Anika?" Not waiting for a response, John then said with something almost like fear in his voice, "I'm going to try to find a vine or something to help pull you back up." John called down to me and then vanished back into the brush.

Looking around my surroundings and trying to figure out what to do, I then decided to skirt the nettle patch to find another way up when I found myself face to face with a tall, dark-haired man who wasn't John or a guard.

In absolute panic, I screamed, "JOHN!" at the top of my lungs as I back peddled and landed on my butt back in the middle of the nettle patch. "Not again!" I grumbled at the ground. Looking back up at the man, he seemed to be in shock just as much as I was.

"I'm Mika, let me help you out of there. I mean you no harm." He extended his hand to help me out of the mess I found myself in again. I took his hand reluctantly, but the honest concern in his eyes made me want to trust him.

Taking a moment to really look at him, I realized he was actually wearing civilian clothes, not the military-issued clothes that I had grown so accustomed to see. He had to have been around twenty years old, but I could be wrong; he had a timeless look to him. His deep blue eyes continued to bore into me before I finally spoke.

"Thank you," I said, still embarrassed and worried about this stranger. Once on my feet, I said, "You scared the crap out of me." I absentmindedly began rubbing and itching my severely stinging skin with the back of my sleeve. "Where did you even come from?" I stuttered as I began working the sleeve of my jacket over the sores on my face. They were beginning to become more and more painful as the moments passed.

"I live not too far from here." Hesitantly, he then added, "I didn't mean to startle you; I'm not used to having people out here." He was still eyeing me in curiosity as he answered my questions and then asked one of his own. "Are you all alone out here? I think you screamed a name, but I haven't seen anyone else but you."

"No, my friend, John, was up on the ridge over there." I pointed in the general direction that I had last seen him. "That is, before I fell down here." I then began looking around even more anxiously searching the ridge for my friend and becoming even more worried as the time crept by without a word from him.

John

I should have paid more attention to our surroundings and seen the unsteady ground before Anika had fallen. I began beating myself up as I scramble trying to find something, anything to help Anika. I swiftly began searching, finding a stick here or a vine there, and then immediately tossed them after a short survey, finding them to be inadequate to pull Anika's weight.

Getting more and more frustrated with myself, I was supposed to be protecting her on this quest of ours, but here I am, and she is down there, in a stinging nettle patch of all things.

Subconsciously, I realized that I was putting Anika in my mother's shoes and trying to protect her like I couldn't protect my mother. I need to give her more credit. Anika really is nothing like my mother. She is strong, smart, and so very capable of taking care of herself.

After I began giving myself a pep talk about how I needed to separate these two very different women, I heard Anika scream my name with complete fear in her voice. I began hyperventilating, with flashbacks of my mother crying my name as my father was attacking her. I pulled myself together and began running in the direction of the ridge.

Once at the top of the hill where Anika had fallen, I witnessed her back peddling and then tumbling back into the nettle patch as a tall man was walking towards her. I saw the man extend his left hand, not in an aggressive way, but to help her up. She reluctantly took his hand and began speaking to him. I couldn't hear what they were talking about from up here, but it didn't appear that he meant her any harm. I was still going to be on guard.

At that moment, I had bound down the ridge in protective mode, the way I should have been when my father was attacking my mother, only to find Anika and this unknown man having a conversation about me.

Then her eyes met mine. "John, oh thank God! I was worried about you!" She ran and nearly knocked me over as she hugged me. I pulled her back just a little to take inventory of her injuries. She had what looked like painful little red sores in streaks all over her hands and face, but other than that, she seemed to be in one piece.

"Are you okay? That looks like it is super painful..." I pointed to what looked like the worst of the sores on her cheek.

She tilted her head up and said, "Nah, just a little scrape. I will manage." I could see that she was trying to be strong, but the tears that were on the verge of escaping her eyes said it all.

I then turned my attention to the unknown man standing near

us and said with the most intimidating voice I could muster, "And you are?"

Anika

I hadn't realized how worried I was about John until just that moment. He was my best friend, and I would truly be lost without him. Untangling myself from around him, I backed away, slightly embarrassed that I had nearly mauled the poor guy. I was just so happy to see him.

I turned to Mika and began introductions, "Mika, this is John. John, this is Mika." Then looked at John and said, "He doesn't live too far from here, and he has invited us back to his village to regroup. He even offered to feed us!!" That last part wasn't supposed to sound so excited, but I couldn't help myself. I was very hungry, and the bitterroot was not something that can sustain a person.

"We should go. We need to get some medicine on your wounds before they get infected." Mika said, matter of fact. "Our elder, Quipe, has a special ointment that can take away the sting and reduce the redness. She will want to speak to you both." He turned and began walking towards his village.

Apprehension was written all over John's face. "Are you sure you can trust this guy?"

"I honestly don't know, but I do get a feeling that he wants to help." With that, John took my lead, and we followed Mika out of the forest.

Chapter Sixteen

Within the small clearing Mika had brought us to, several larger yurts were erected in a semicircle around a fire pit. There were a few people rummaging around, preparing food, making what looked like clothing, and a few small children playing tag. We received some concerned looks from the villagers, but they kept their heads mostly down and continued their work. Still following Mika, I nearly stumbled right into his back when he stopped abruptly in front of one of the yurts with an open door.

"This is Quispe's tent. I will go in and let her know of your arrival. Please wait here." Then, he entered the yurt.

"John, I know that we are capable of doing this journey on our own, but I think we need to take help when we can get it." I whispered just over my shoulder. "I think they are just as wary of us as we are of them. Look at their clothes, then look at ours. We look more like guards than they do. I can understand why they look at us with such fear."

"I didn't think of it like that!" John began peering around at our surroundings in earnest. "I think you are right. They're trying to keep their heads down and acting as though nothing is wrong, but the fear in their eyes is totally giving them away."

I chose then to allow the eavesdroppers to hear me. No longer whispering, I said, "Six days of walking has felt like an eternity. The emotional rollercoaster that this journey has put us on has been insane." Taking a deep breath, "First of all, we come out here completely ill-prepared for what we would see, and second, what we would need for supplies and for rations. We didn't even think to bring near enough for the trip there, much less the trip back." Frustration starting to show on my face, I said, "We need to take a moment to regroup, rest and restock before moving forward. I know we can't afford the extra time, but we need to do something…" Rubbing my sleeve on my face again, I wince. "And maybe some medicine?"

John simply nodded, rubbed my shoulder, and said, "You are right, Anika. I am sorry that I do not have the faith in people that you do. I have been scared for so long that it does not come naturally to me to trust people." He then ran his hand across his face in disappointment.

"It will all be okay, John. I promise. I have faith." Trying to sound as confident as I could, which wasn't easy. Knowing John's background made it so that I understood where he was coming from, but it didn't make the show of confidence manifest as I needed it to.

"Well, I have faith in you, so for now that will have to be enough." He looked down at the ground and skid his boot in the loose soil in contemplation. "For what it's worth, I am sorry. I didn't think that it would take this long to get to where we are going, so I didn't plan better."

"This isn't all on your shoulders! I assumed we would have been there already, too, but we didn't anticipate the struggles we've had along the way. We should have but didn't." Taking on the most optimistic view I could, I said, "We will make it! We will get there and get what we came out here for and get back to Mr. Boss before you know it."

"I hope you are right…" was all John said before Mika and Quispe came out of the yurt.

The old woman, and I do mean old…she had to have been

in her late sixties. I had not seen a single person over forty in almost seven years, and I was taken aback by her fragility. She was much shorter than I am, standing somewhere around four-foot-eleven. Her silvery-gray hair was pulled back into a long braid, well past the middle of her back; her deep brown eyes were filled with worry, and the wrinkles around them showed her age. Mika had a protective arm around this fragile woman. When he looked at her, you could see all the love in the world shining through his eyes. True love and affection passed between the two before she turned and spoke to us.

"Good morning, my name is Quispe. I am the elder here in the village. Mika has told me that you are in need of some assistance. We do not have much but what we have is yours." She gestured to the expanse of her village.

"Thank you, Quispe, for your kindness and generosity. My name is Anika, and this is my friend, John." I gave a small bow to her.

With a nod to the two of us, she then addressed the rest of her people, or at least the ones that were in earshot. "These young travelers are weary. We will do what we can to assist them. They mean us no harm. Please tell me, who of you will feed and house them for the night?" She looked around, with my shoulders slightly bent so, as not to appear imposing.

"I will." A short, stalky female raised her hand.

"Thank you, Tala." Then she turned to address John and me. "Go with Tala, she will get you settled. I will go fetch the necessary herbs for your wounds and meet you shortly. Rest. Eat." With that, she walked back into her yurt with Mika at her side.

"Come. This way." Tala ushered the two of us to a yurt not too far from Quispes'. "We don't get visitors often. Please forgive us for being so suspicious of you. Your clothing looks like the guards, and any interaction we have had with them has not been good."

Tala opened the door to the small yurt and the smell of something sweet blew past us. It was a familiar scent, but I could not quite place it. The yurt was decorated with warm colors, dried plants hanging all around, and fur pelts lining every flat surface. She motioned for us to have a seat in one of the four woven chairs against the wall.

"We honestly understand your feelings toward the guards. In our region, civilian clothing is not allowed. Everything we have is government issue. Which is why we look like them, but I assure you, we are not guards." I placed my pack on the floor next to the chair Tala had instructed me to sit at when my bag fell open, and one of the pamphlets fell out.

I was thinking hard about how to breach the subject of the rebellion when Tala surprised me and said, "I know that pamphlet…" just under her breath.

"I know you do not know me and therefore do not yet trust me, but I ask you in earnest, do you follow the rebellion?" I hoped that I had not come on too strong and that she might open up to me, I then said, "I am the one that made these pamphlets and started the distribution of them…"

John looked at me with concern in his eyes, and, as if I could read his mind, I heard him say, "Are you sure you want to divulge so much information?" I nodded at him that things were fine.

Tala then spoke. "I do not believe that a guard would be carrying so many of these pamphlets around with them as you are. I believe what you say."

Taking the deepest breath, I had taken in what felt like days, I began to relax. "Thank you for your trust. I know it is difficult in these dark times to trust a stranger."

"I believe you, not because of the pamphlets or even your words, but in the way you carry yourself. You truly believe what you say, and it is obvious to anyone with eyes. Your compassion for those around you shines bright and you have a way about you that breathes integrity into everything you speak." She nodded gently, then said, "We must get you well so you can continue your mission."

No longer lingering in the corner, John finally spoke up and said, "We have poorly planned our journey and ran out of rations quicker than anticipated. If you might help us replenish our stock, that would be the most immediate need." John spoke in a quiet voice; admitting his wrongs was not easy for him. I put my hand on his, trying to offer what little bit of reassurance I could give him, as he was being humble and respectful, even though he was still leery of asking for help from strangers.

Tala turned her head to John and nodded slightly. "As Quispe stated, we do not have much for winter will be upon us soon, but what we have to spare is yours."

Just then, the door behind John opened, and Quispe, Mika, and another man entered the small yurt. "I have with me, Mika, who you know, and this is Keokuk. He is our scout." Keokuk was very tall and wide. Even though his stature was extremely large, he moved and held himself like a much smaller man. He appeared always watchful and on guard but moved quietly and quickly. "He knows these woods better than any of us. John, if you, Mika, and Keokuk would step outside the yurt, you can discuss a plan of action while I tend to Anika's wounds."

I could tell that John was not comfortable being separated from me, but I just gave him another small nod and said, "If I need you, I will shout."

"Okay," was all John said in reply and followed the other men out of the yurt.

"I did not feel it appropriate to have the men stay, so I thought Keokuk would help your John settle a little. He seems very on edge. From what Mika told me, I can understand why." Her voice was like a soothing grandmother as she said, "Okay, young lady, I must ask you to undress so I might see the extent of your injuries."

Shyly, I did as I was told. Removing my military boots and folding each item as I took off my clothing, I placed them on the chair next to me. My whole body ached, but every place the stinging nettles had touched burned and itched excessively. Once I was standing in just my undergarments, I saw the extent of the damage. There were sores across my lower back where the backpack had not been, around my lower stomach, up and down both arms, and all over my face and neck. Basically, everywhere from my waist up. I also had a few scratches and bruises on my legs from where the branches of trees and bushes had brushed as we had walked.

The old woman grabbed me by my shoulders, twirled and twisted me around, looking me over, then twirled me around again. When she had finally gotten a good inventory of my injuries, she said, "Okay, my dear, this will be uncomfortable at first." She explained what she was going to do. "But it won't take long before the herbs will begin their work and sooth these sores. How exactly did you come by them?" I felt true concern in her voice as she began sticking her arthritic fingers into the salve she intended to slather all over me.

"I fell down a hill. The ground was unstable and corroded under my feet. I landed at the bottom of the hill in the middle of a stinging nettle patch. Once I freed myself from their horrible grip, I fell back into them when Mika startled me." Recounting the facts, my cheeks became very red with embarrassment. "I did this once before when I was six, I think. My mother put me in a bath of calamine lotion."

"Ah, I see." She just nodded in complete understanding as she began wiping the cold herb salve on my sores. Her fingers were cold and rough against my hot, sore skin. At times, it almost felt like she was rubbing sandpaper against my skin. Once the ointment started to soak in, it truly did feel so much better. "You should be able to breathe now, my dear. It should not take but a day or at the worst case two days to completely heal." As she rubbed, she made idle chit-chat, talking about this or that, mostly things that had no consequence. Her soothing voice was beginning to lull me to a restful state, so when she abruptly stopped rubbing and said, "Okay, now we must feed you," she had startled me awake. Turning to Tala, she said, "Tala, can you please give our young friend a few items of clothing for the night?" After she turned back to me, she said again in her sweet voice, "We need to wash your clothing. The stinging nettle has soaked into your clothing and, if it is not washed away, you will get more sores."

In complete understanding, I nodded to her and thanked them both for every kindness they had bestowed upon me.

John

Being sent out of the yurt by an old lady that reminded me of my grandmother made me feel slightly uneasy, but as she was not at a Deaders camp, I decided I should trust her because she was wise enough to escape the guards and stay safe. I followed Mika and Keokuk into another larger yurt. This one was not decorated quite as nicely as Tala's. It appeared to be set up as male housing, with more masculine colors and décor.

Mika plopped down on one of the cots and motioned for me to sit in the chair beside it. "Have a seat. The girls will be a while; let's talk."

Keokuk sat in the adjacent chair and shocked me by saying, "Where are you two headed? By what I have witnessed, you are on a mission and are not guards, so should I assume you are part of the revolution?" His voice was grainy and sounded almost as though he didn't use it much.

Looking at him, almost like a dear in the headlights, my mouth gaping open, I finally was able to get out one word, "Yes."

Mika leaned forward on the cot and said, "If you are part of the revolution, then what is your mission, and what is it that we can do to help?" Mika then said, "There may not be very many of us, but we are willing to do whatever we can."

I sat there in shock that Anika's instinct was spot on about these people. "I should start by saying to you that I was completely against coming here and trusting any of you. Anika is an amazing person, and she believes that most people are innately good. I grew up in a world where I felt quite the opposite. With that said, you have shocked me with your willingness to help our cause without knowing any real details." Looking from one man to the other, I continued, "We are on our way to Headquarters. Anika's mother, who has escaped from one of the Bio Camps, has sent word that there is proof of the wrongdoing done by the Protectorate in Headquarters. She has instructed Anika to steal this proof and distribute it to the masses, ultimately bringing down the Protectorate from power."

Keokuk looked like he was deep in thought before he finally said, "Okay, so now we know why Anika is on this mission, but what is your role in all this? Why are you with her?"

"Yeah, what has made you want to join in this?" Mika's voice sounded almost accusatory.

I felt I needed to be completely transparent, "Anika is my best friend, and I would do anything for her. I came along for two reasons. One, to keep Anika safe, and the other is while at Headquarters, I need to find a missing girl's whereabouts to rescue her." Putting my face in my hands, I continued in a low voice. "I was paired with a girl named Vicki. She and I really hit it off, that is, until we received a letter telling us that our pairing had been severed. Vicki was then taken to a holding station and eventually taken to a Bio Camp to extract some rare antigen."

Keokuk bowed his head to me and then said, "Your honesty is much appreciated and your reasons for doing this is valiant. I will help you."

"As will I!" Mika blurted.

Chapter Seventeen

That night, the village sat down for a communal meal, which consisted of REAL FOOD! Salmon that was roasted over the fire, wild asparagus, fresh fruit, and boiled potatoes served with homemade bread. All the fruits, vegetables, and meat were all harvested from the surrounding area.

John and I ate like starving children, stuffing our faces, barely using our utensils. The villagers made sideways glances at us as we ate but did not say anything about our ravenous behavior.

Once we had finally slowed our eating and realized how extremely ill-mannered, we had been, I apologized for our behavior, stating, "This was the first real meal that John and I have had in almost eight years." Looking around at the table full of wonderful food, I continued. "The rations we get in Area 12 are mostly for nutritional purposes only. Either powdered, freeze dried, canned, or pressed. Not much of what they give us is fresh or tastes good." Taking a deep breath and looking as appreciative as I could, I said, "We thank you so much for opening your home. This has truly been a blessing to us both," John only nodded through bites but did not say anything, "We will cherish your kindness forever!" I could feel my cheeks heat up as they all just looked at me without saying a word, and I felt as if my embarrassed rambling fell on deaf ears.

Finally, Quispe put me out of my misery when she spoke up from the crowd and said, "We do understand. Some of us have come from other regions and know exactly what you say of the rations they provide. We hold no judgements. It is okay, my child, eat. We have much to discuss once we are finished here, and the light is fading." With that warm, grandmotherly smile, she put me at ease yet again. While we finished eating, I could hear the villagers talking about the tasks that needed to be completed for tomorrow. They were mostly discussing harvesting more food for winter; how they would stalk pile and preserve it for the long cold months. I got caught up again with the delicious food and ate until I was more than full.

With much convincing, John and I helped the villagers clean up after the meal. The villagers had a difficult time allowing "the guests" to assist in the nightly chores. We cleared and washed plates from the meal and helped to package what was left of the food; thanks to John and I, there wasn't much left. We shuffled around following orders from Tala and a few of the village women, doing whatever was asked of us.

After everything had been done, John and I were then ushered into the largest of the yurts by a shorter, balding man. "Wait here, you will be met shortly by Quispe and the others." He gently closed the door behind him.

Standing just inside the yurt, I turned to face John as we waited. I saw apprehension in his eyes, but he didn't voice any of the concern written on his face. Abruptly, the door came open and bumped a jar on the floor, rattling the contents in such a loud unexpected way that it caused us both to jump nearly a foot off the ground.

Seeing the frightened looks on our faces, Quispe said, "Easy, my children. All is well." She slid into the room with such grace and ushered us to the center seating area of the yurt. Keokuk moved into the room just behind Mika and Tala, closing the door and posturing himself as the protector of his elder.

After we were seated, Quispe gently placed her apparent age worn hand on top of mine in the grandmotherly way she did, calming my nerves and relaxing the room with such ease. "We," Quispe motioned to the three villagers who were with us, "have taken a moment to discuss your situation. We have agreed to help you on your quest. Mika and Tala have both requested me that they be allowed to accompany you and to assist you with the journey. I will allow it." She waited only a moment to see if there would be any reservations being voiced, but there were none. I wanted to hear them out completely, without interrupting, before I opened my mouth.

Keokuk said in his gravelly voice, "I will also be accompanying you. I have more knowledge of the area and know of several safer routes to get to Headquarters." In the matter-of-fact way he spoke, there was no room for argument; Keokuk would be going whether we wanted him to or not at this point.

Even with all their faces on mine with expectant looks, all I could do was stare back at them in shock that they were willing to go with us. I lifted my head and tried to appear confident in what I was about to say; I spoke to all of them at once. "Though we do appreciate all you have done for us thus far, we could not ask this of you! It will be dangerous, and I could never think about putting any of you in harm's way! You all are such wonderful people!" I was nearly in tears with the thought of these strangers being willing to risk their lives for a quest that wasn't even theirs!

"I would have to agree with Anika with this one. This is not something we have jumped into lightly and jeopardizing yourselves is not necessary. The rations and supplies that you have already sacrificed is more than enough!" John turned to me, put his hand on my shoulder, and said, "We will only ask that when you meet others, speak of the revolution and speak of hope for a new future."

Tala then stood up and spoke firmly, "This request was not made lightly. We have lost loved ones in this, and we want to do our part to change things! We will be going with you; there is no question in that." Quispe grabbed Tala's hand and pulled her back to her seat.

"We may only be a few, but we have felt this war more than most. The three people you see before you, have the means and abilities to help you. It was only a sign of respect that they even asked me if they could go because, truth be told, they would have gone anyways. This cause is not just your own. Please, remember that, young ones." Quispe looked at me with such grief in her eyes when she said, "I had five children and was married for many years to the love of my life. All of them have been taken by the protectorate. There is not much an old woman can do for the revolution, but I can spread the word from here. These young people can help you along the way with their strong backs, immense will, and kind hearts, if only you open your eyes and see it is not just you who are taking this journey."

I looked around the room and back at John, nodded to him and said, "I do not believe I am alone in this, so many have been lost..." I trailed off for a moment, thinking of my parents and wishing with everything I had that they were here with me. "We only have a crude plan, but here it is..." I pulled the maps and my mother's letter from my bag and showed it to them all. I explained everything I knew so far and resigned to trust these people with everything.

Keokuk looked over the maps while Tala and Mika looked

over my mother's letter. Keokuk began to get a sly grin on his face when he abruptly said, "I can get us to Headquarters in a day, maybe two, by my route, and if this Matt guy's intel on the guard shack is accurate, then we will have proof in hand in three days!" Keokuk sounded triumphant in his analysis.

While John and Keokuk discussed the route and supplies needed for the trek, Tala, Mika, and Quispe were asking me questions about my mother's letter. They answered a few of the questions I had about the letter and told me of things they had seen and witnessed in the real world.

As the light faded and candlelight became dim, Quispe quieted us all, "Children, it has become very late, and you all need much rest for your journey. I think a solid plan has been set into motion and you will succeed." Getting to her feet with the help of Tala, Quispe pushed us all to the door. "Go, sleep. In the morning, I will have the others gather supplies for you, as you get the rest needed for such a journey." Just before we were all out the door, she reminded us where we would be sleeping. John with Keokuk and Mika, and me with Tala. She was still very much a proper lady and wanted this village to observe what was proper.

We walked quietly so as not to disturb the other villagers. The moon was bright and high, which made it much easier to make it to our designated yurts. Once we got to the men's yurt, John bent down and hugged me gently and said, "Please get some sleep, if you need me, I am just a holler away." After releasing me and walking into the yurt, I stared after him for a moment, feeling grateful to have him as my best friend, then continued walking to Tala's yurt.

Tala opened the door, and again my senses were overtaken by the sweet smells wafting toward me. She milled around the small space for a few moments, returning to me with bedding. She made a make-shift bed by one of the side walls for me out of thick pelts and soft fluffy pillows. The bed was so luxurious and warm, which was a stark contrast to the bed at the barracks that were draughty and bumpy. She then handed me the softest fabric sleeping gown. It had been the most comfortable item of clothing I had felt in all my life.

After I was all tucked in and, feeling like a queen, I lay there staring around the room, taking in the many sights that I did not catch when I was in here before, all now illuminated by the small flickering candle on the nightstand. The wood carvings strewn all around, the ornate tapestries lining the walls, and all the different dried wildflowers hanging around the roofline. Tala's house was warm, comfortable, and inviting. The familiarity of the scent finally hit me; it was the smell of the honeysuckles that were dangling not too far from my bed. When I would visit my grandmother's home when I was a child, these grew like weeds in one of the fields by her house. "Tala?" I said quietly.

"Yes?" She rolled over in her bed to face me.

"I have been laying here wracking my brain, trying to figure out why your house smells so familiar, and I finally figured it out!" With a small amount of excitement trickling out of my voice and a reminiscence that was almost tangible, I said, "When I was a little kid, I used to visit my grandma's house. She had honey suckles that grew all over around her house. She and I would spend afternoons picnicking in the fields, and hours picking honeysuckles for decorations inside the house."

"It sounds like very fond memories. I am glad I could aid in recovering small part of your youth." You could hear the smile in her sleepy voice.

"Sleep well, Tala. Thank you again for everything!"

“You are so very welcome.” Tala then rolled back over to her side, and, within no time at all, I could hear her soft, steady breathing of sleep.

With the sounds of Tala sleeping around me, exhaustion overtook me, and I drifted off into a deep, dreamless sleep.

Chapter Eighteen

John

After looking in on Anika for the umpteenth time, I resigned to help out wherever I could since sleep did not come easy for me. Though the bed was comfortable, and the sounds of the guys' snoring was a normal sound I was used to back at the barracks, it was difficult to shut my brain off. I did everything I could think of to fall asleep, but it was just not happening.

I left the guy's yurt well before sunrise and began getting firewood for the main cooking pit. Once the villagers started rousing, they were able to give me directions of things to do to occupy myself.

I was sitting in front of the fire in the wee hours of the morning, staring into the embers, thinking of all that needs to happen in the next few days to have everything run smoothly. Mentally creating plans for the backup plans, so in my own world, I became startled when Keokuk patted my shoulder and said, "Good morning, friend. Did you not sleep?"

"Not really. My mind was too busy racing through all the things that could go wrong to get much solace," I admitted more to myself than to him.

He wore a look of complete understanding, which in some ways surprised me, just as much as when he patted my shoulder. "Let me tell you something not many know about me." He then sat on the log across from me and began warming his hands in front of the fire. "This village is not my home, though that is public knowledge. I was taken from my home and family by the Protectorate at the age of thirteen, and they 'enlisted' me into their Guard. They said if they got us early enough, then the 'brainwashing' would take much easier." Taking a deep breath, he continued on, sounding more gravely than before. "The Protectorate injected all of us kids with chemicals to 'help' us grow." He put little air quotes around the word help and grimaced. "Then, more chemicals that were designed to create muscles and strength, all while we were indoctrinated into a vast variety of fighting classes, studying strategies and other things to create the 'perfect soldier'.

"I knew about the Guard camps, but I was under the impression they were true Volunteers, not, well.... *Volunteers*." I had been looking back and forth from the fire to Keokuk as we talked. If I had not been paying attention, I don't think I would have seen the vulnerability that rolled across his face just then.

"Yeah, well, that is how they make it look, but I can tell you that is NOT how it is." He didn't take his eyes off the fire. "I was in their service for five years until I witnessed firsthand what the camps were really like. I could not continue turning a blind eye to what they were doing." The firelight glistened in his unshed tears. Keokuk blinked them away as fast as they appeared and continued to explain. "At dead of night, I escaped from the Protectorate and ran. I ran and ran until my feet could no longer hold me and I collapsed from exhaustion and dehydration. While I was unconscious, Quispe found me, brought me back here and nursed me back to health. If it were not for her, I would be dead and so would so many others in this village. We owe her our lives."

"Then, why are you going with us? You should stay and take care of your village, not walk into certain death." I was dumbfounded by this man sitting in front of me. He had been through so much, and he was willing to jump right back into the fire.

"It is the right thing to do," is all he said. We sat there in silence for about an hour before he got up and stretched out his stiff muscles and said, "Come on, we have work to do."

Anika

Waking up disoriented, with the sun glaring in my eyes through the small windows of the yurt, I looked around and found no sign of Tala; her bed was made, and the room was picked up.

I folded the bedding that Tala had lent me and placed it at the end of her bed. Then, reluctantly, I changed out of my soft sleeping gown and back into my scratchy clothes. Tucking my things back into my military issue bag and, with it firmly placed on my back, I ventured out into the bright morning.

As I made my way, I saw the villagers busily going about their day, doing what I would assume would be their normal. Mika was distractedly stocking the fire pit while talking to a slender, pretty, dark-skinned girl that looked to be close to his age. He had a light in his eyes and a smile from ear to ear on his face when he spoke to her. I wondered if there was a relationship between the two of them. I made a mental note to ask Mika about the girl.

No Pairing stations way out here in the woods, so the idea of having a relationship grow organically was appealing. Thinking of the Pairing stations brought me back to Steven. I have grown to appreciate him and look at him fondly, but do I think there could be more between us? I don't know. Does he even think of me like that?

"Anika, you're awake!" Mika yelled. "Great, let me get you

some food. Almost everything is ready for us to leave." Mika had caught sight of me and ran up to me like an excited dog catching a glimpse of his owner, rambling and nearly jumping up and down with excitement. "John and Keokuk have already gotten the supplies together, and Tala has been working with Quispe on preparations for warmer clothes since winter is coming quicker than we thought."

"Why didn't you guys wake me up earlier?" In complete annoyance and still sleepy, my voice came out much squeakier than the firm and frustrated that I had intended. So instead, I put my hands on my hips and just glared at him.

"Well, John said that it had been over twenty-four hours since you guys had gotten sleep, and he said we needed to let you rest. That guy really cares about you and was only looking out for you and your well-being! Don't be mad," he said with his hands up and in a defensive pose, backing away slowly as if I was an angry momma bear and he was in the way of my cubs.

"Fine," was all I could muster, but I knew he was right. I needed the rest, and John was only trying to help. "Where are the others now?" I said with a much more calm and nicer tone.

Finally taking his hands down and back to his sides, he said, "We are all supposed to meet with Quispe once you had gotten up. So, I guess that would be now…." He trailed off in thought. "Go to Quispe's yurt and I will round up the others, okay?"

"Okay. Thanks." I nodded my acknowledgment.

"Oh, and when I come back, I will bring you some food, too." He had said over his shoulder as he was briskly walking in the opposite direction.

At Quispe's yurt, the door opened just as I approached, "We've been expecting you. Come in." A shorter, boxy female waved me into the yurt. At dinner the night before, this girl had sat not too far from me, and I think she introduced herself as Jennifer, but I could be wrong. I am not good with matching names with faces. Good thing that was not part of my job back at the region; otherwise, I would have been fired a long time ago.

"Good morning, my child. I hope you slept well." Quispe warmly greeted me as I walked into the yurt. Standing with her arms open wide, looking expectant for me to come running for a hug, I reluctantly and obediently obliged. As her arms enveloped me, all the emotions of the last five years seem to just flow out of me. I missed my mom so much, and being wrapped in this woman's arms was the closest to a mother's hug I had. I began to sob. When I say I began to sob, it was that ugly, snotty, air-gasping sob that almost causes you to hyperventilate. It came out of nowhere, embarrassment written clearly all over my face as I pulled away from her.

"Don't worry, everyone has that reaction with Quispe." Jennifer handed me a piece of fabric for my face (not just the tears, snot, but also the drool that had escaped from my open crying mouth). "The first night I came here, I laid here in her lap for almost a full twenty-four hours just crying. I was like a small child who had gotten hurt, and momma was there to sooth the ache." She soothingly rubbed my back as I blew my nose and caught my breath.

"We all need a good cry every once in a while, dear, nothing to be embarrassed about. It is good for the soul, and, with what you are about to walk into, you needed a good soul clearing cry before the battle." She then handed me a cup with some warm liquid in it and motioned for me to drink. "It is a tea. I make this tea to strengthen the body and energize the mind."

I Smelled the warm vapours coming from the cup, "It smells

slightly of the nettle patch and of lemons." She took another long breath before taking a drink.

"You have a good nose, my child. Nettle and lemongrass tea. It is a detoxification tea. It flushes the stress and cleanses the body. This will also help to increase your energy, kind of like a natural coffee substitute." She gave a little wink at the coffee part. "I am going to send a bag with you that has herbal medicinal remedies and organic first aid items in it. It will come in handy, as well as some more of this tea."

"Thank you for thinking ahead like that. I honestly hadn't thought of that part of the trip. We really could have used your herbal remedies when John ate too much of the knotweed." I gave a disgusted look to emphasize and give serious impact to my words.

"OH MY!" Jennifer said from behind me.

"Yeah, it wasn't pretty." I gave a small giggle.

"You have no idea! It was way worse for me!" John said from the slightly ajar door. My cheeks pinkened and then turned flame red.

"Sorry, John, we were just talking about herbal remedies… I wasn't making fun, promise!" She tried hardest to back pedal just a little.

"No, you're good, Anika, you were right, it was bad!" John gave a small shudder in remembrance, "With that being said, Keokuk and I have planned a lot better when it comes to rations, so that kind of thing shouldn't happen again. Hopefully!"

"Glad to hear it!" Then, turning to Keokuk, I said, "Thank you, Keokuk, for all of your help. It is greatly appreciated." He just gave a small grunt and nod in my direction.

With Mika finally joining us, we all found our respective places around the room and sat down to discuss the final details to the plan. Mika slid a plate full of food towards me, fresh fruit, scrambled eggs—the real stuff, not the powdered, dehydrated kind, and some more of the fresh warm bread the villagers make. I was so delighted to see the plate; I wrapped my arms around Mika in a huge hug before I began devouring my food. I only added nods or grunts to the conversation happening around me as my mouth was crammed full of food.

After all the final details had been solidified and my stomach was full, we began saying our "see you laters" as Quispe did not want to hear a goodbye, for it was too final for her taste. My bag had been unpacked and repacked with the right items and slapped back on my back. The others did the same, and, just as we were about to head down the path, Quispe called out to me, "One more thing, my child."

"Yes, Quispe?" She stood expectantly in front of her.

"This is for you. It was given to me by my late husband, and I want you to have it." She grasped my hand and slid a beautiful ring onto my right ring finger.

"I cannot accept this." She said, by looking down at the rose gold band with the "We are Mighty, We are Strong" engraved on the exterior.

"It is a match to your bracelet and to your necklace. I'd say it was meant to be." Quispe gestured to my jewelry, "I saw them when I was aiding you with the nettle stings, I knew this little thing," Twisting the ring round my finger, she said, "belonged to you."

"Thank you, Quispe, I will think of you whenever I look at it!" I said, by giving her a big bear hug.

She then bent me down just a touch so that she could kiss my forehead. "You are strong, and you will succeed, my child, take care!"

"You as well!" I waved and began down the path toward my destiny.

Chapter Nineteen

Diary Entry Anika's Mother, Jeana

February 12th, 2056

Matt has been visiting me regularly, making sure that I am getting something to eat and taking care of myself. Because of the chemicals the Protectorate gave me, the green illuminated veins are now spreading down my arms, legs, and up my neck. I have gotten to the point that it has become difficult for me to move; my joints lock up, and the pain is nearly unbearable.

Until today, Matt was okay with me staying on my own, but when he saw the extent of the disease and its growth, he relocated me immediately to a "Safe Cell". These are places that are free of the Protectorate and their Guards...for now.

On the way to the "Safe Cell", he told me of the revolution gaining in strength. He also told me the part my amazing Anika has had in the growth of the revolt. Of the pamphlets and wall art being distributed through the regions. I could not be more proud of her!

Fear has become crippling me in the last weeks, and I begin to think of the worst things... What would Anika think when she sees me like this; would she run in fear like the children here in the Safe Cell? Will she even find me? Will she get here in time? Or will I die before I look upon her face one last time?

NO! I will not think like this. I must think POSITIVE! She is so much stronger than she knows; she will succeed! She will get the proof needed, and she will find the cure I so desperately seek!

She will!

Chapter Twenty

Keokuk was in the lead, guiding us up a mountain face that had a livestock path and not much more. With my motley crew in tow, Keokuk did little grunts here and there, pointing to guard shacks in the distance, then continued on. "If we stay on this course, we will skirt right past them all. I know it's a harder path, but it is much safer."

We all did our best to keep our voices down and keep the pace, but there were times climbing up the mountain we would slip, fall, or get hit by branches and cry out. As the road became narrower, we started walking in a single file line. First was Keokuk, Tala, John, me, and then Mika taking up the rear. Keokuk was so much more equipped to deal with this than any of us, having the strength and endurance.

Again, I felt more and more out of my element as we followed Keokuk up this blustery thoroughfare. The only thing that kept me going was knowing we were only a day away from getting what we came out here for.

John looked over his shoulder at me, "You okay?" he looked a little concerned for my well-being.

"Yeah, I'm good. A little tired but good. You?" I said, slightly breathless.

A little winded himself, he said, "Doing all right. Hopefully we find a clearing soon so we can rest."

"I agree with that whole-heartedly!" Talking was making it even harder to breathe as we trekked up the mountainside, so the rest of the walk was spent in silence.

The ground turned to mud as we got closer to the summit. It had been raining, and that did not make the travel easy. My boot caught the slimy side of a smooth rock, and I went tumbling down the path and right into Mika's rescuing arms. "Thanks, nice catch."

Keokuk saw what had happened and yelled down the narrow path, "You guys okay down there?"

To which I replied, "Yea, Mika's my hero!"

Mika's voice trembled when he said to me, "Yeah, just be a little more careful on the rocks from now on. I was afraid I wasn't going to catch you."

"I'll do my best, but those rocks have it out for me...." I tried to make a bad joke to take the heat off but didn't succeed.

After what felt like two days of climbing the mountainside, Tala startled us all. "A clearing!" Tala said excitedly

"We will rest for a bit under the branches of that tree just over there. We need to dry off a bit and get some food." Keokuk looked soaked to the bone and just as tired as the rest of us but too much of a "soldier" to admit it, blaming the group's need for a break for the reason we stopped and not admitting he needed the break as well.

Mika spoke up first. "Should we start a fire or are we too close to the guard shacks?"

"We are in the cloud line. I think it is safe to light one but not a big one." John said as he looked to Keokuk for confirmation.

"Yeah, that should be okay." Keokuk disappeared into the brush for a few minutes, and when he returned, he said, "We should make camp here; the wind is starting to pick up, and we do not want to be caught on the backside of this mountain with rain and wind." Gazing towards the sky with concern in his eyes, he then looked at Mika and the rest of us and said, "On the way down, the rocks will be just as wet, and with the wind pushing us off our balance, we could really get hurt. We don't really need any more help in that department." With that, Keokuk just gave me a sideways glance.

"Yeah, the rocks were bad enough on the way up here, as Anika found out." Mika turned to me and gave a small, little, sly grin in my direction to let me know he was just picking on me, too.

John and Keokuk gave each other a knowing look when John said, "Anika, I might put a rope around your waist for the trip down. You are great on even ground, but I don't want to lose you over the side of the cliff again!" He sent a smile my way.

"Ha ha, very funny guys! I am not that clumsy...." Trying to say it with a straight face was near impossible. "But that rope idea, I might take you up on that."

Tala just sat under the tree, giggling, as the guys picked on me for being clumsy. Then she decided to pipe up and mention, "Well, sweetie, you did fall into a stinging nettle patch, not once, but twice...I think 'Clumsy' is a very appropriate nickname for you!"

I just grumbled and finally gave in. "All right, you got me there...." I began thinking about falling down that hill and into the nettle patch. "That really hurt, by the way!"

"I can only imagine," Mika said. "I really am sorry I scared you so much you fell *back* into them!" He emphasized the word 'back' and then giggled some more.

"All I can say is thank God for Quispe and her miracle cream! Otherwise, I would still be a blotchy, stinging mess!" She put out another silent blessing for meeting Quispe. "Well, I'm glad that you all find this so amusing." I was thankful that there was a little lighthearted humor, even if it was at my expense.

That night we spent laughing and telling jokes to each other. It was a nice evening, and if this had been before the war, you would have assumed that we were just a group of friends out camping. We ate curled up under our makeshift tent by our firelight and promptly fell asleep.

I dreamt that night about walking on a tight rope made of stinging nettle vines. I was not able to stay on the vines and fell down into a rushing river of calamine lotion and then landed on a beach filled with slippery rocks. Between the mud and the rocks, I was completely unable to keep my balance, falling on my butt over and over while listening to the laughter in the wind. I was then running on a muddy treadmill being chased by military boots. Everything then went black, and I fell into a dreamless sleep for the rest of the night. When I awoke, everyone else was milling around and packing up.

"How'd you sleep?" Tala asked me when she realized I was now awake.

She remembered bits and pieces of her dream world, "Weird dreams but otherwise, I slept okay. How about you?"

She shrugged her shoulders, "It was okay, but you were whimpering in your sleep, and that was kind of distracting."

Embarrassment flooded my cheeks. "I was? Really? I am so sorry for keeping you up!"

"Yeah, what were you dreaming about anyways?" Mika came over to the tent. "You were kicking the crap out of me…"

"Oh, my goodness, I am so sorry!" I said, absolutely mortified. "Basically, the short story is, I was dreaming about stinging nettle tight ropes, rivers of calamine lotion, slippery rocks, mud, and military boots. It was really bizarre, but I guess with all the joking around last night about my clumsiness I can understand most of the dream."

We picked up camp and quickly began down the mountainside. The ground had dried a bit from all the wind during the night, so the trip down was much easier than we anticipated.

"Hey John, I guess the waist rope wasn't necessary after all!" she threw a little elbow jab at John when they got to the bottom.

John said with a little laugh, "The day is still young, Anika."

"Quiet guys!" Keokuk said in a whisper and made a cut sign across his neck. He crept forward into the brush and disappeared.

"What's going on?" Tala whispered.

"*Shhhh*!" Mika put his finger to his mouth.

Everyone was on guard, looking around expecting the boogie man to jump out of the bushes, when Keokuk came back and said, "We are in the clear. I heard a guard's radio and had to investigate. Anika, can you pull out that map of Matt's? I need to see how far off we are from his instructions."

Taking my bag off my back and positioning it on a nearby downed log, I rooted around inside until I found what I was looking for and handed both maps to Keokuk. "Here you go."

"Thanks." Keokuk sat on a nearby downed log and began investigating the maps.

Chapter Twenty-One

Breaking into Headquarters

"Ok, we are here." Keokuk pointed to a spot-on Matt's map. "There is a small guard shack over here," he pointed not too far from where he indicated they were standing. "I am going to sneak into the guard shack and grab a uniform and radio, which will make it easier to get into headquarters itself." He then turned to face me. "Anika, since you know what documentation we are supposed to be getting out of there, I think I will need to get a uniform for you as well. What size do you think you are?" He seemed to be sizing me up and taking a mental inventory.

"Maybe a medium? Not sure really..." I shrugged my shoulders.

"Got it." Keokuk Nodded in understanding. He then turned to the group and said, "We will only have about twenty minutes max in the building since shift change only lasts thirty minutes. There will be less guards on duty."

John then spoke up. "Being an ex-guard, you know their routines. Is there anything we need to do while you and Anika are in the building?"

Keokuk thought a moment before he replied, "Fifteen minutes after we enter the building, I need you guys to cause an explosion near this guard shack." Keokuk pointed to another spot on the map but this guard shack is closer to Headquarters, "Create a diversion large enough to get Headquarters' attention and allow us time to escape." Keokuk then put his hand on John's shoulder and said, "Just don't get caught! That would really complicate things!"

"Agreed!" Mika and Tala said in unison.

John then began to fidget and said, "But how am I supposed to do that exactly? Are there explosives in the guard shack or something like it?

"There is a backup generator in each guard shack. If you stick a piece of fabric in the fuel tank and light it, that would cause enough of an explosion to catch their attention, but once you light it, RUN as fast as your feet will take you."

"Okay, I got it." John nodded.

Keokuk looked at us all and said, "All right, everyone wait here while I go get the uniforms and radio. I will be right back. Stay down and out of sight." He turned and stalked off in the direction of the first guard shack.

As soon as Keokuk was out of sight, we hunkered down and waited patiently, though impatient for him to return. "I don't really know if I'm ready for this…" My voice started to tremble a little. "Now that we are here, it has now truly become real!"

Tala wrapped her arms around me, enveloping me in a long hug. "You've got this, sweetie! We all have faith in you! Just do the best you can."

I decided that while we waited for Keokuk to return, I would reread my mom's letter and make sure I knew exactly what paperwork I need to get.

Steven

It has been nine days since John and Anika left on their mission. I have nearly paced a hole in my office floor and bit the head off most of my staff. I am beginning to get really worried about their safety. "I really hope they didn't get hurt or worse get caught." Pacing and talking to myself became my normal. "I should have gone! God, I hope Anika is okay!"

I was startled by a knock on my office door. "Yes, what is it?" Steven's voice still sounding gruff and rude.

"Sir, I come bearing news." Matt peaked his head through the large office door.

"Oh, Matt, please come in!" excitement oozing from me. "Close the door behind you."

"Yes, sir," Matt said respectfully. He closed the door and stalked over to the chair that had been placed in front of my desk. Matt was still standing, refusing to sit.

"What news have you brought me?" I Hoped it was about Anika and John, but it could have been any number of things since Matt was the mail carrier for the Protectorate.

"Sir, we need to talk somewhere else," Matt said, looking over his shoulder with a strong sense of paranoia coming from him. "This is not for everyone's ears."

"Okay, there is only one place I know of that we can talk freely. Follow me." My chest became very weighted with anticipation for the news, so I quickly stood and motioned for the door. I'd take him to the old barn that Anika and I found.

As we left my office, I had to address the needs of four different staff members before Matt and I could get out of the building. I know I did not handle the staff very well; I was just too anxious to hear what Matt was going to tell me. I can't apologize to these people for my bad behavior because that would contradict the image that I have to portray for the Protectorate, but I hate it; this is not who I am.

Once Matt and I finally made it to the old barn and were situated in the seating area that Anika and Steven made, "Okay, this is a safe place to talk."

"All right, Anika made it clear that you are on our side, and I can trust you, but I am still very leery. I am trying to be transparent here. I do not want any one to get hurt, especially Anika." Matt made his voice sound very intense to get his point across.

"Anika doesn't know it, but I am in love with her. I don't want anything to happen to her!" I hadn't admitted that to anyone, much less myself, until it just slipped out of my mouth. I carried on, saying, "Which is the reason I have been so mean to everyone the last few days. I am worried sick about Anika, and John too, but mostly Anika."

"Fair enough, I wouldn't be at my best if the person I loved was in a dangerous situation." Sliding his fingers through his tousled hair, he then continued. "Okay, here goes. I have secreted Anika's mother to a Safe Cell. The Protectorate had her in a Bio camp a few years ago. She escaped and has been living in gutters and abandoned buildings until I ran into her. They used her as a pin cushion, injected her with all kinds of different chemicals, and she is fading fast now. She wants to see Anika before she dies. Is there any way you can make that happen?" Matt pleaded with Steven, begging for mercy.

"Of course, I would do anything for Jeana. She was always a kind woman to me. Only problem is, Anika is not here, and I do not know how much longer this mission is going to take. I don't even know if she is alive, or if she has been captured." At this point, I stood up and began pacing back and forth, worst case scenarios running through my thoughts again without any sign of them ceasing.

"Well, there is something that I can do. I am the mail carrier, I can go to Headquarters and find out the status." Matt looked slightly hopeful, "I could see if they have even made it to Headquarters yet."

Stopping in my tracks and turning to Matt, Steven said, "That's right, you have your scooter and could get there pretty quickly." I turned around and began rubbing my scruff, thinking. "Okay, go to Headquarters. I will send you with a quarterly report, giving you a reason to be there. After you have gotten as much intel as you can, come back here and let me know what you've found out!" I was getting anxious for this plan to be put into action; I started walking towards the door to the barn.

Matt stood up abruptly and followed me back to the office to get the quarterly report.

John

Keokuk returned from the guard shack quicker than we anticipated. With uniforms and two radios in hand, he addressed the group, "We will turn these radios to channel two. That is a station that is not used; we will each take one. When Anika and I are in the building, I will give you a signal. At this point, you will start the count down." He stopped in his explanation to make sure we were all on the same page, then continued, "Fifteen minutes, no more, no less. The distraction has to go off without a hitch, or Anika and I will be caught!"

"Got it!" Understanding rolled through the group.

I knew my role in this, but I was so afraid that I would screw up and everyone would get caught. It must have shown on my face because Anika came over to my side and said, "You okay?"

Unable to look into my friend's eyes, I just say, "When we are all at the rendezvous point, then I will be okay, but not until then! There is so much that can go wrong between now and then! I know I play a pivotal role in your escape and that scares the crap out of me! I don't want to disappoint you!" John shook his head back and forth, "I couldn't live with myself if you got hurt, Anika!"

She wrapped her arms around me and gave me the warmest hug I think I've ever gotten in my life, and said against my chest, "John, we aren't alone in this anymore; we have help. I will be safe and so will you!"

"Ah, guys, don't get all mushy now. We have work to do, save that for the rendezvous point!" Mika teased.

Anika released me then and gave my arm a small punch. "Go blow stuff up!" and she walked into a nearby bush to change into the guard uniform.

Anika

I now look at John like a big overprotective brother, and I couldn't be happier. Knowing he has my back is making this mission much easier to bear.

As I stepped out of the bushes in the guard uniform that Keokuk gave me, I felt a bit like an imposter but reminded myself, "This is for a good cause. We could save millions when we get the proof we need."

Keokuk got everyone's attention and addressed the group in a very matter-of-fact tone. "All right, everyone knows their part. Does anyone have any last-minute questions or need to say anything before we get this plan in action?"

Chapter Twenty-Two

Anika

As our group began separating, the weather changed from the rain and fog to snowflakes that poured down on our heads.

"Well, this may help us stay hidden," Mika said to my back.

I turned around to face him and said, "We can only hope!" I made a silent prayer for my friends and my safety.

Keokuk gave me a small tutorial on how to act, walk, and talk before we left the break in the tree line. As an 'Underling,' I was not to speak unless spoken to, be a presence but really nothing more, outwardly, that is, but inwardly, I was to pay close attention to exits and how many other people are around us. He said, once we got into the building, "I will talk to the other workers and distract them long enough for you to sneak away to get the documentation." Or at least, that was the plan.

John

After hearing the signal on the radio, we found the Guard Shack with ease and, just like Keokuk said, there weren't any Guards. The generator was chained on the left side of the building.

Looking around the Guard Shack for something, anything to stick into the fuel tank, but coming up empty, I decided I'd rip my jacket into a long strip of cloth and use that to ignite the tank.

Counting down the fifteen minutes since we heard the signal come through on the radio made me feel like an eternity had passed. Stress and anxiety ran through our small group as the clock timed down. I unscrewed the fuel tank lid on the generator and started feeding the fabric strip down into the tank, leaving a good twelve inches sticking out the top as a fuse.

"Did you want us to do a ten-second count down to lighting the fuse?" Mika looked at me once I got the fuse in place.

"Yeah, that wouldn't be a bad idea," I replied.

Tala just nodded as we spoke but began fidgeting with her hands and nibbling on her lip as the anxiety about what we were about to do grew.

"Ten…nine…eight…" Mika and Tala said in unison as I grabbed the matches out of my pocket. "Seven…six…five…" Their voices trailed off in my head as I positioned myself in the best way to light and run.

"TIME!" they said, louder than they should have, but I lit the fuse either way.

We began running back towards the tree line. When I looked back at the shack over my shoulder, it was still standing, and no explosion happened. I stopped running just shy of the trees. "What?"

"What's wrong, John?" Tala looked back at me when she realized I was no longer running.

"It didn't explode!" Fear coursed through my veins. "What are we going to do now?"

"There must have been diesel in the tank instead of gas! We've got to get Anika and Keokuk out of there, NOW!" Mika said, coming back and joining Tala and me.

"Oh, my goodness, what are we going to do? We don't have time for this nonsense!" Tala's voice was trembling.

"I've got it!" Mika began running back towards the shack, opening the door so hard that it slammed into the wall behind. He then tore through the desk and grabbed a bunch of the paperwork and the wooden chair. He then ran outside to where the generator was and began making a teepee style fire between the generator and building. Catching on to what he was doing pretty quickly, Tala and I went into the shack, grabbing everything we would find that was flammable, and brought it to Mika. We got going the biggest bonfire we could. The hotter we could get the fire, the quicker the generator would go up in a beautiful ball of exploding flames. We hid the generator in all the debris, with the chance that Guards could get most of the fire under control, but the generator would still blow. With the side of the building now on fire, the smoke began rolling.

The snow continued to dump on us, but that didn't stop the fire from growing; it only caused it to billow and roll. We ran for the tree line again. We then watched from far as the shack was engulfed in flames and smoke.

We hunkered down in the bushes at the rendezvous point, hoping that this was the distraction, our friends need to escape.

Keokuk

Being back in a Guard uniform made me sick to my stomach, but if this is what it took to stop The Protectorate from hurting any more innocent people, I would do anything.

As we were walking up to Headquarters, I began getting flashbacks of my time in service; some would say I have Post Traumatic Stress Disorder, if you subscribe to that notion, but I don't want any such label.

I watched what The Protectorate did in the Bio Camps. They showed no remorse for giving normal healthy citizens horrible, deadly diseases that killed them in slow, gruesome ways. No mercy.

Being forced to aid in bringing in the victims to their

inevitable deaths was not what I signed up for. I thought I was helping to keep the peace until I was stationed at the Bio Camps.

I got close with one of the captives; her name was Jeana. She was the nicest, sweetest woman I had ever met. It was the last straw for me when I watched how my fellow Guardsmen treated her like a rabid dog and began shooting her with a tranquilizer gun from outside the cell they kept her in. It was at that point I made the choice then and there that I would help Jeana escape this hell.

After I read Jeana's letters and realized who she was, it warmed my heart and soul that I was helping her yet again but this time, through her daughter. Now, as I walk through the doors of Headquarters with Jeana's daughter by my side, furthering the cause of the revolution, I feel a small amount of relief. I may yet atone for my actions.

Chapter Twenty-Three

Keokuk

After we got into the building without really being noticed, Anika and I got close to the targeted office we needed to be in, when we were confronted with a group of four Guards talking. I took this as my chance to engage them in a lengthy discussion about protocols to allow Anika the chance to slip into the office relatively quickly.

These four Guards were all fresh out of training, and this was their first station. Though I am only twenty-two, I am a veteran in the ways of The Protectorate Guard, and speaking to these young men who appear to be no older than seventeen was making it very easy to convince them that I belonged there.

I mentally returned to the village as the young men spoke and thought about how hard it had been for the villagers to believe that I was only eighteen when I arrived. The severe dehydration caused my voice to permanently become a gravelly and gruff sound. I give off a vibe of a much older, wiser man than my age would normally portray. People automatically assume I am much older than I really am. The life I lived as a Guard made growing up much quicker through brainwashing and intense training; childhood was a thing of the past.

I was brought back to my current surroundings when I heard a large BOOM not too far from this building. John had done it! There was our distraction and our way out of here. Quickly, I turned to the four young Guards and said, "Per Protocol 16-2 you need to begin escorting all personnel out of the building and bring them to the safe zone. You get those people over there, I will go over here and get anyone else that might be in the back offices."

"Yes, sir!" With fear very apparent in their eyes, they seemed relieved to take orders rather than have to think about what to do next.

Anika

After I snuck into the back office my mother indicated on her map, I saw a long wall full of file cabinets and immediately became discouraged. As quickly as I could muster, I began going through drawer by drawer, looking for anything that looked like the right documentation, feeling like this was a needle in a haystack situation. My internal dialog kept on playing havoc, the entire time.

"No, this isn't it!"

"Nope, this isn't it either!" "Dang it, I'm never going to find it!"

Just as I was truly losing hope that I'd ever lay hands on the proof of what The Protectorate was really up to…Eureka! I found three files crammed full of important-looking documents. A loud noise I could only assume was the explosion John, Mika, and Tala were supposed to set went off. I heard people screaming from the other room, "FIRE!"

In the pandemonium that followed the explosion and fire in the Guard Shack, Keokuk burst into the office and told me in a very hurried voice, "Get out of the Guard uniform. I have to get you out of the building like you are any other employee. Hide the documents on your person so that you aren't holding anything as we walk out of here."

All I could do was follow the instructions I was given as quickly as humanly possible.

Matt

Showing up at Headquarters just as a large explosion went off, all hell broke loose in the building. Guards were pulling people out of the main building and dragging them off property to what they were calling, "To safety." As I watched the scene unfold before me, I witnessed a taller Guard holding Anika by the elbow, dragging her out of the building. "She's been Caught!" I said under my breath. "I have to tell Steven!" I turned and left as fast as my scooter could take me.

Stay tuned for the conclusion of this epic tale in book 2 of Deader's Day.

Deader's Day Book 2

PREVIEW:

Anika's Dad, Alan

Feeling like I was standing there looking through the eyes of a stranger at the situation in front of me, I just stood there in shock. How could this be happening?

I am staring down at this woman I don't even recognize anymore. She is beaten, broken, bruised, and bloody. Watching her shudder in pain and sobbing uncontrollably, my heart ached for her, but so many people have said she has done this to herself. I am not so sure about that, though.

I never imagined that this would be the way I would see her again...